DRAGONS SKY

NOAH HARRIS

DRAGONS SKY

PARANORMAL SHIFTER – M/M NAVY SEAL BOOK 4

NOAH HARRIS

Disclaimer

This is a work of fiction. Names, places, characters, and events are all invented. Any similarities to real people, places, events, living or dead are all unintentional.

This book contains sexually explicit content that is intended for a MATURE AUDIENCE ONLY.

DRAGONS SKY

Arulean Black has never quite been the same since the wars that devastated dragon-kind, decimating their numbers and forcing them into hiding. He lost many loved ones and watched the weredragon race crumble, all the while unable to stop these events from happening. With the distance between him and his mate further than ever, Arulean lives as a shadow of his former self, drifting from one day to the next and haunted by the guilt of their history. When the last of the Elders dies, Arulean decides it is time to call for a Summit, a meeting of all the dragon kings across the globe, to determine what their future will hold. He is determined to keep the peace, while his mate tries to rally support for revenge. The problem? He feels like a living ghost. What he doesn't expect? To meet a young omega with fire in his heart and heat in his eyes who makes him feel alive again.

Rajiah Bronze has never quite felt like he belongs. He's never appreciated the company of other dragons, and despite his mother's urging, never felt the desire to have a mate. He's all but convinced he doesn't want one. He spends most of his days traveling the world and living among lesser shifters. He finds their presence much more calming than that of dragon-kind. However, when his mother dies, he's given the task of bringing her ashes to the Summit. The problem? His older sister is pressuring him to find a mate. What he doesn't expect? To fall completely head-over-heels for the powerful and elusive dragon king, Arulean Black.

There are certain lines they shouldn't cross, but those, coincidentally, are the exact lines that might be worth crossing after all.

CHAPTER
ONE

Her scales were a blood-red mark against the orange-stained sky. The sunset cast the world in warm hues, reflecting off the clouds in splashes and colors that complemented her own colors perfectly. She twisted mid-flight, catching the winds, wings expanding and carrying her higher and higher. She pulled them in close again and, diving toward the lake below, expanded her wings once again sailing across the water, sending ripples in her wake.

It looked as if nature was nothing more than a backdrop to her beauty, for beautiful she was, with a strong, powerful, aura cascading off her in waves. Her body was lithe and slim and quick, muscles coiling and rippling beneath her scales, body twisting and writhing in the air, wing movements precise and graceful. She looked as if she commanded the wind instead of riding on it, as if the world bent to her and her alone.

And, once upon a time, he supposed it had. As she rose high again, soaring over the valley below their castle, she let loose a roar. It was primal, emotional, and full of a raw anguish that tugged at his heart, adding to the sharp sting of his own pain. He could practically feel it rip from her jaws, tear past the tissue, hear the blood in her throat. Dragons couldn't cry tears in their beast forms, but that didn't mean he couldn't hear the sentiment.

His chest felt hollow, his heart pricking pain with each beat. He felt it pulse through him, oddly dull and muted. He knew of sorrow, and that's what this was. He felt it in a deep-seated weariness in his bones and the sluggish way he moved. He felt it in the heaviness of his thoughts and how his stomach rebelled against food. He felt it in the way despair seemed to cling to and claw at his flesh. But all those sensations were dim compared to what they once had been.

At one point in his life, just a few centuries ago, he would have felt them strongly. He would have been up there with her. He would have roared his pain and lost himself to the winds in a flight of mourning. He would have joined her, and they would have intertwined their bodies mid-flight, sharing pain and taking comfort in each other.

But now, he was numb. He knew his sorrow was deep and strong, but he felt detached, as if he was watching and feeling his sorrow from high above himself, as though it couldn't quite touch him. The fact that he felt anything at all was proof enough that this sorrow was shaking him to the core. It was leaking out of a place inside him, deep down where he buried these feelings, the deep pit of despair that he kept hidden and buried, lest they make him crumble. For he knew that if he actually let himself feel, if he let himself mourn every time they lost one of their own, he would crumble. And if he were to crumble, their kind would truly be lost.

So, he kept his sorrow to himself, he put up a strong front. He had to be strong for himself, for his people, for his mate. She writhed in the air, ruby scales flashing like fire in the light of the setting sun, silently calling out for him to join her, to mourn with her.

He remained where he was. They hadn't mourned together in centuries. She was a wild creature, prone to emotions and instinctive reactions. Her wildness had once been something he admired in her. He'd loved her fire, passion, and strength. Now he saw them as weaknesses. He saw her flaws, the way her rashness could hurt them. Her emotions controlled her, and that wasn't a quality befitting a leader. Not the kind of leader their people needed. If she couldn't be that person, he would have to be. If they both fell prey to their emotions, then surely everything would be lost.

So he let her mourn, but he didn't join her.

He watched her flight long into the twilight, long after the sun set and the moon began to rise. He watched her body twist and writhe, heard her screams and cries, heard as sorrow gave way to anger, and then give way to sorrow once again.

He was never particularly close to his mate's mother, and from what he'd known of Lyphnia, neither was she. But her mother had been a prominent figure among the weredragons, an alpha female and a strong leader, and one of the last known breeders. In fact, she was widely recognized as the Great Mother after having given birth more often than any female or omega dragon in history. She had been incredibly fertile for one of their kind, and as such, she had dedicated her life to being a breeder, a title that was increasingly rare among weredragons, whose birthing rates were very low; therefore, anyone able to give birth and keep their species alive was highly regarded.

She continued to give birth long after most dragons would have been considered infertile. She had been a miracle and a blessing among their people. And now she was gone.

She had also been one of the last of the Elders. Those belonging to the previous generation of weredragons had been alive for several millennia and helped build their power around the globe. The greats had established their power before passing on the world to their children. Lyphnia's mother had been the last breeder among the Elders, the generation that was more fertile than his own. She had been nearly six thousand years old when she died. There were a few other Elders alive, but no one quite knew where they were. They had long gone into hiding, choosing to live out their days in solitude, apart from shifters and humans alike. They became hermits, removed from a society that had long since passed them by, waiting in peace until their own passing.

The Great Mother had been the last Elder active in dragon society. With her death, all of dragon-kind felt a loss, a sense of abandonment, hopelessness, and of knowledge that new times were indeed here. They had all felt the passing of time and the changes since the war and the purge, but this was a confirmation of the new age. Their last ties with the past were severed. This was no time for uncertainties, but decisiveness.

And it was time for Arulean to assert his authority once again and truly bring his shattered people back from the brink of extermination, to keep them safe and ensure their survival.

He turned away from his mate's mourning flight, ignoring the dull tug in his chest as he turned back to their castle. He strode through the dark, stone corridors, letting the familiar chill seep into his bones and bring with it sharp clarity.

The Great Mother's death was a long time coming, and her life had become one of the biggest roadblocks in his striving for peace. Without her in the way, he could finally put safety precautions into place, and work on saving his people. His biggest obstacle now was Lyphnia, his own mate and very much her mother's daughter. But she could be controlled and kept in check. Her wild emotions and rash decisions could be reined in as long as he kept their mateship bond intact.

They may not have shared a bed in several centuries, he may not feel more for her than a sense of nostalgia and bitter resentment, and she may hold little more for him than nostalgia and thinly veiled contempt, but he would hold their mateship bond strong.

For the good of his people, his own happiness could be sacrificed.

After all, it was his fault they were in this situation to begin with.

"Sire, the queen approaches." The dragon spoke softly, bowing respectfully to Arulean's back.

Arulean hummed his acknowledgement, but did little else. He remained where he stood, next to the large lodestone, hands hovering over its surface but not touching. He could feel its power humming in the open air, an increasing pressure in the space between them, like static aching to spark. He kept his eyes closed as he spoke, "Thank you." Truth be told, he had felt Lyphnia's presence nearing them long before the announcement. "You may leave us."

There was a hesitation. "Sire..." the man said, his voice uncertain.

Arulean opened his eyes, half-turning to look at the man. He stood tall, as most dragons did, but it was more due to his presence than stature. He wore the robes suited to his station, black with gold and silver markings. His hood was down, and the tattoos that adorned his shaved head were visible, runic markings disappearing down his neck. As the keeper of the lodestone, his status was high, but he was weak in comparison to Arulean's aura. Not even he was above a king.

Still, Arulean understood his hesitance. His job was to look after the lodestone, after the ashes of their ancestors, to keep the connection between them all open and active. He was loath to leave anyone alone in the chamber, especially if that person's temper was as volatile as Lyphnia's, and especially given her less than stable emotional state.

Arulean gave him a small smile, a mere quirk of the corners of his lips, and tried to soften his gaze enough to convey understanding. "I will keep her under control. You have nothing to fear. As well, I do not believe either you or your acolytes will want to be around when she is here," he said, not unkindly. It wasn't a warning or a threat, just a statement of fact. Her sharp tongue was well known, and her courtesy did not extend to those she considered beneath her, which consisted of anyone without dragon blood. And Jorra's acolytes were all shifters of other breeds. Gone were the days when there were enough dragons to hold all the positions.

Arulean, personally, saw no issue with having lesser shifters around. Most of those who worked in the castle and lived in the small village below were refugees, come to seek shelter and safety with the dragons, away from humans. Arulean couldn't turn them away. As long as they bowed to his rule, he had no reason to.

Lyphnia didn't necessarily agree, but she had no argument against it. Their own kind became rarer and rarer by the year, and if she wanted to remain in power, she had to extend her influence to others. Lesser shifters had always been under their rule, but there had always been enough dragons for her to ignore them completely. Now, not so much.

Jorra chewed his lip in thought, looking over Arulean's expression before pursing his lips and bowing his head. "I entrust the cavern and the stone to you then, sire." He took several steps back before turning on his heel and striding away. As Arulean watched, he gave a sharp gesture in the air, and several others in similar robes stepped away from their positions along the walls, slipping into double file behind him as they left the cavern and headed deeper into the mountain's cave systems. Arulean didn't blame their hasty retreat. As reluctant as the man had been to leave, he knew that no one was particularly fond of being in an enclosed space with Lyphnia. The dragon queen had a reputation, and she hadn't been the same since the purge.

Once the keepers were gone, he turned back to the lode-stone. A large black and gray stone, centered in a massive cavern deep in the heart of the mountain. The roof of the cavern rose high, its ceiling disappearing into darkness. The chamber itself was wide enough to fit a score of dragons in their beast forms, the walls cut naturally from the stone. They were dotted with small holes and pockets, nearly invis-ible from a distance as they blended into the uneven surface. Each hole housed the ashes of one of their kind: their ances-tors, their brethren.

The entire burial chamber practically hummed with an ancient and nearly untamable power. The presence of so many all around him, as if watching him from the afterlife, waited and judged his actions. He stood with his hands sweeping over the lodestone, never quite touching the surface. It was a conduit of their blood, a way to amplify their aura out through the ties that bound their kind, a way to send out a call. But he couldn't do it alone.

He felt her presence as she descended before he felt the

reverberation of her landing through the rock beneath his feet. Moments later there were footsteps, muted but echoing around the cavern walls. He listened to her approach through the long hallway leading to the burial chamber. Her steps were slow and measured, as they always were. She had always been one for making people wait and making sure that they knew she was doing it on purpose. It was one of the many ways she commanded power. Just as it was one of the many ways that she attempted to assert authority over him. It never worked. He was a patient man who refused to fall prey to her antics.

Once upon a time they might have been endearing. Now they were just another of her flaws.

"You didn't join my flight last night." Her voice rang out, even and calm, but as chilly as the mountain air. She paused in the entryway. Her aura was strong, easily drowning out the dull, faint pulses from the holes in the walls, but barely touched his power.

"I prefer to mourn in private," he said with the same amount of ease.

"You didn't before," she pointed out coolly.

"True," He said simply. She was right. Once, when they were young and close, when their kind were at their peak, they would mourn the loss of one of their own together. They would fly together, entangle in the skies, and share in their grief by celebrating the living. But that was before death became commonplace and before he started to blame her for the deaths. "But it has been centuries since then. Now I prefer to mourn by myself."

"You didn't fly at all."

"Flight is not necessary to mourn."

"It is to release the sorrow."

"It was not necessary."

"You don't allow yourself to feel enough."

"You allow yourself to feel too much."

Silence. A standstill. One they had come to countless times before, and one they wold no doubt continue to reach. He took a step back, half-turning and looking at her for the first time since she'd arrived. She stood tall and proud, poised and dignified. Her hair was the same deep red as her scales, dark in the dim lighting of the cave. Her features, like most drag-ons, were sharp and angular--ethereal. Her eyes were dark, limpid pools that he knew would glisten like blood in the light. Her human body was curvaceous, indicating the fertility that she had once embodied.

She was beautiful in an otherworldly way, just as she was terrifying. He had once been drawn to her flames. Now he realized that fire was cold enough to burn.

He held out a hand to her, a peaceful gesture, one that would allow them to move past their impasse. "Come," He said, voice low and kind, with a gentleness that was almost foreign now. "We must make the call."

Her lip curled in a small sneer, but she stepped forward, practically gliding across the floor to take his hand. "What do you plan to achieve, Arulean?" she asked, curiosity softening her tone. He tugged her forward by the hand, and she moved automatically to stand next to him in front of the stone. "You have called a Summit at the death of every Elder, and yet nothing has changed. Our kind remains at an impasse. We are independent creatures, Arulean. To try to unite us under one is a fool's errand."

"It once wasn't so," he said mildly, lifting their joined hands to the stone, hovering close. He closed his eyes, lifting his chin as he felt the hum of power surround them. When he spoke again, his voice was soft, almost a murmur to himself. "Once, we could and did, unite in packs as other shifters do. An Alpha to rule and Elders to guide."

She scoffed, but her tone was sad. "That was when our kind was powerful and plentiful. When we were powerful. We are no longer seen as the king and queen we once were."

"Perhaps, it is time to reclaim that title."

"Perhaps ..."

Together, they reached forward, palms touching the surface of the lodestone. Sparks of power arced toward their flesh, electricity running up their arms. The low hum of power around the room intensified, and Arulean felt his own aura spread. He felt it surging out from him, mixing and mingling with Lyphnia's familiar power. For once, he didn't shy away from it. He embraced her aura, letting it combine with his own to increase their influence. He felt it spread outward, catching on the faded presence of their ancestors and kin, amplified by the lodestone, pushing outward. Beyond the cavern, beyond the mountain, beyond their castle, and beyond their valley home. A flare, big and bright, shooting out and calling, blood to blood.

He knew the others would feel it, wherever they were. With every dragon who felt it, it would surge through them, renewing and reinvigorating, and move on to the next. It would crackle and spark through all of them, like a net of lightning connecting their kind, invisible to the naked eye but powerful all the same.

They would answer the call. He had once been a king, chosen by the Elders. They may not bow to him anymore, if they ever did, but they would come. The last of the influential Elders was dead.

For better or worse, it was the dawn of a new age.

CHAPTER
TWO

Rajiah was an impatient yet patient man. When it came to arrogance and violence and fear-mongering, he had little patience. When it came to alphas and elders, he had little patience. He didn't like being told what to do, especially when it went against everything he believed to be right. He hated waiting for changes to be made. Perhaps that was why he had never really gotten along with his own kind. With a lifespan of several millennia, dragons were notorious for being stuck in their ways, allowing stubbornness to carry them through until everything crumbled around them. As it had.

When it came to children and the nature of continuously and persistently asked questions driven by a healthy curiosity, Rajiah had all the patience in the world.

"What's the castle like?" the young girl asked.

Marli sat on his shoulders, her small chubby hands buried in his hair. She couldn't be much older than eight. So young and so innocent, barely a seedling in this world. She had grown on him in the weeks he'd spent traveling with her pack. It had been ages since he had seen a dragon so young. They aged normally in adolescence and then their metabolism slowed greatly in young adulthood, creeping forward with such sluggishness that it looked as if they never aged for centuries. That, combined with their dwindling birthrate, meant he hadn't seen a dragon child in several hundred years.

"It's big," he said, gesturing grandly with one hand. "Huge! Carved right into the side of the mountain, with a whole village and a lake in the valley below."

"Is it pretty?" she asked, voice hushed in awe.

"Very," He said with more certainty than he felt.

Truth be told, it had been years since he had been there. Years and years and years. Almost five hundred to be exact. The last time he had been there, he had gone to visit his older sister after presenting as an omega. He hadn't wanted to, but his mother had insisted. It was their effort to showcase him to the world as an eligible young omega. He had hated it. He had spent most of that time hiding, running from his responsibilities, and causing enough general mayhem that no alpha in his right mind would want him.

Much as he had spent most of his life, if he were being honest.

"Will we see dragons?"

"Am I not dragon enough?"

She scoffed. "You're not a dragon, dragon," she said in that matter-of-fact way that only children can.

"Is that so?"

"Nope."

"And why is that?"

He felt her shrug on his shoulders. "Because you're always down here with us. You're not up there!" He tilted his head back in time to see her waving a hand in the air.

"I prefer it down here."

"Why? You have wings!"

"Because I'd rather spend time with you."

She giggled.

"Why don't you fly though?" asked her older brother. Regge was a young man trapped in the gangly phase of post-adolescence: limbs and hair too long, awkwardly skinny, and looking like he was trying to fill shoes that didn't quite fit yet. He walked beside them, hands behind his head and fingers laced together, stride casual and confident. He had recently presented as an omega and was still coming to terms with how his role in his pack had shifted. He put on a strong front, a brave and cocky demeanor, to hide his uncertainty at seeing his alpha peers beginning to treat him differently. Lately, Regge had taken to spending the traveling days with Rajiah and Marli.

"Don't you like flying?" Regge continued. "If I could fly, I don't think I'd ever want to walk again."

Rajiah shrugged, jostling Marli and making her screech with joy. "I do. Flying is an amazing experience. I've spent months in near constant flight. But... it's dangerous now. Humans aren't afraid to hunt us. We have to be careful." He glanced sideways, giving the young man a sad smile. "Besides, flying can be lonely."

Regge looked away, teenage face scrunched up in thought.

Marli bounced on his shoulders, tugging at his hair. "I wanna see a dragon fly!"

"You've seen me fly."

"I wanna see more!"

He chuckled. "You will." He understood her awe. It wasn't common to see his kind anymore. Considering the much shorter lifespan of other shifters, most of them had spent their entire lives without ever seeing a dragon. It was a sad thought. Still, at The Summit, Marli would be able to see plenty of weredragons. Not nearly as many as there once had been, but definitely more than she would have ever seen otherwise. "The Summit brings dragons from all over the world. You will see many scales and shapes and sizes."

"What is The Summit?" Regge asked, side-eyeing him. "I've heard you talk to the pack leaders about it. What's the big deal? A bunch of dragons meet up?"

Rajiah eyed him, an eyebrow raised in mild amusement. "The big deal is that we are mostly solitary creatures. We do not live in packs as you do. Our kind lives spread out across the world, and it is only during a Summit that we all gather. Summits are only called after the death of an Elder or in times of great need. It is when all important decisions about our kind are made."

He still remembered the call. It had come several days after his mother died. No doubt Lyphnia had felt their mother's passing. Blood called to blood, and the immediate blood between parent and child was strong. Rajiah had been with her when she passed. It had felt like a part of him had been ripped away, leaving something cold and hollow in his chest. He wouldn't have been surprised if all of dragon-kind had felt something wrong that day, but her children would have felt it more deeply. Lyphnia would have known exactly what it had meant.

That was probably why The Summit had been called so soon after her death. The last time an Elder died, it had taken weeks for a Summit to be called. News had to travel by word of mouth and messages. This time, there was no need.

Lyphnia and her mate had been the ones to send the call, as they had been for the past several Summits. He had felt it like a wave of lightning, singing through his blood and crackling across his skin. He had felt the pressure of their combined aura flood through him, a wave of power and demand, a call that only dragon-kind could hear.

He had resisted the call for years and avoided The Summit. He had no reason to believe that he could make a difference. Dragon-kind were obstinate and set in their ways. They had been at an impasse since the Great Purge, and they would continue to be so. Going to a Summit meant being around his kind. It meant seeing the dwindled numbers and feeling the pressure of his secondary sex. As an omega, he had a duty to breed, to keep his kind alive. Or at least that was what his mother had believed. He didn't want that duty and had never asked for it. The best way to evade the alphas that would try to claim him was to eschew The Summit altogether.

Unfortunately, this time, he had to go. The call was a song of home and family. He couldn't have resisted the call even if he tried. Besides, he had been the only dragon kin with his mother when she passed, and as such, he had to deliver her ashes to the burial chamber.

"What is it this time?" Regge asked, drawing him out of his thoughts.

"Hmm?"

"The death of an Elder or a time of great need?"

Rajiah felt his expression darken as he whispered, "Both, I'm afraid..."

"Will they really be able to give us shelter?" the boy asked, voice quiet and uncertain.

Rajiah gave him a sharp nod, eyes fixed on the horizon ahead. "They will." Packs and shifters of so many species had been flocking to Arulean and Lyphnia's kingdom for years, especially recently, with the increasing expansion of humans, the evolution of their weapons, and the inflated self-righteousness they had about purging anything considered inhuman. He knew of his sister's stance on lesser shifters, but he also knew that she had yet to turn them away when they came to live in the valley beneath her castle. He wasn't sure if that was because of her own need to rule over people, or Arulean's influence. He didn't know much of the man anymore or where he stood. He supposed he'd find out. "They will," he repeated with more conviction. "I'll make sure of it."

They were close to the valley when the sickness struck. A mere three days by foot winding through the mountain range, and they would have been safe in the haven that offered food, clean water, and most importantly--healers.

The sickness came on fast, manifesting as a sudden fever in the night. Regge was the victim. He was left in a cart to sleep through the day, his mother watching over him as they attempted to sweat out his fever. By the end of the day, he was much, much worse. Sweat coated his skin, a fever that left his flesh far too hot to the touch. He was flushed, patches of red blotches that blazed with heat all over his torso, arms, and legs. It might have been written off as any ordinary fever had it not been for the massively swollen glands in his neck and wrists.

It was the omega fever. A sickness that wasn't uncommon among young omegas, when their bodies were still changing. Some called the condition a heat gone wrong, the body fighting with itself. It had once been far more severe than it was now. Now healers knew how to cure the sickness quite easily. Without aid, however, there was a less than fifty percent chance the omega would live.

There were several problems. The first and foremost being that the sickness was known to act fast, flaring through the omega's body far too quickly and causing far too much damage if left untreated. They didn't have much time before the damage to Regge's body became irreversible or mortal.

The second problem was that the pack's healer wasn't knowledgeable in treating the omega fever. She was a new healer, having learned what she could from her grandmother before the woman's recent death. The pack was small, a mere twenty-seven weretigers, most of whom were young. They knew how to treat and handle normal fevers, but there was nothing ordinary about this.

The third problem was that they were still a three-day walk from the valley and any possible help. That time could perhaps be cut down to a day and a half if one ran in their beast form and took minimum breaks for rest. But Regge wouldn't survive the journey, and even if a messenger managed to reach the valley, there was no guarantee when aid would arrive.

The fourth problem was one that Rajiah was willing to ignore. However, the pack leaders were not so reckless.

"Rajiah, you can't," the Alpha said, placing a heavy hand on Rajiah's shoulder to hold him back. Physically, the man was much bigger than him, but only in human form, and as a dragon, Rajiah always seemed taller than he really was.

He rounded on the man, slapping off his hand and meeting his eyes with a steady glare. "I can, and I will."

The Alpha didn't budge, eyes narrowing at the corners. "We cannot allow it," he said, pain evident in his voice under the hard edge of stubbornness.

"It's not your decision to make," Rajiah challenged him, standing to his full height, amber eyes blazing as he squared his shoulders. He might have been an omega, and his human form might have appeared younger than the alpha weretiger, but his aura burned brighter and stronger, and they both knew it.

The man flinched. "Please," he whispered, changing tactics, expression pleading. "You cannot."

"If I don't, Regge will die." Rajiah bit out, causing the tigers around him to flinch. He glared at each and every one of them, but none would meet his gaze.

The pack leaders consisted of the Alpha, his mate, and two elders. They all gathered around him, blocking him from entering the tent in which Regge lay suffering. Regge's mother was inside along with Marli, but the rest of the pack hovered a good distance away, pretending they weren't avidly listening to Rajiah argue with their leaders.

"I can't let Regge die," he said, more kindly. "He's still so young. I can save him. I have to."

"But who will save you?" asked the elderly woman. Despite her age, which had wrinkled her skin and grayed her hair, she still stood strong and empowered. Both hands on her walking stick, she met Rajiah's gaze steadily and refused to look away.

"I won't need saving."

"You will, and you know it."

"We don't know if I'll get it—"

"It is known that the fever is only contagious to male omegas. Her voice grew quiet, but no less sharp. She wasn't cruel or unkind, merely stating facts. "It is also known that the sickness is even more deadly in adult omegas. Even with healers, the mortality rate in mature omegas is not favorable."

"That's a risk I'm willing to take," he said firmly, without hesitation. There was no guarantee that he would get the sickness. It would latch onto any omega who handled Regge, yes, but Rajiah was a dragon. He was centuries old and made of stronger stuff than a weretiger. Surely a sickness born in a lesser shifter would have no effect on him. "It's never been proven that the omega sickness from earthly shifters can affect dragons." he continued. "I've only ever heard of it manifesting and spreading from young dragon omegas."

"It's not a risk we are willing to take." It was the Alpha who spoke.

"So you're going to sacrifice Regge for what? For me? You barely know me!" Rajiah lashed out. Every moment they spent arguing was a moment that Regge's condition was worsening. He pointed to the mountain peaks along the path. "This is a three-day journey by foot if you follow the paths. I can make it in hours if I fly. I can take Regge to the valley and get him to a healer. I can save him."

"It is not a risk we are willing to take--"

"That makes no sense!"

"Young dragon," the old woman said, voice calming and commanding respect. Rajiah glared at her, but she didn't back down. He wondered how much of him she could see. Her dark eyes had a milky film over them. "You cannot say with certainty that you will not catch the illness. And if you do, and if you should come to any harm, what do you think will befall us?" She tilted her chin down, keeping her eyes fixed firmly on him. Her tone darkened. "The scarlet dragon's view on earthly shifters is well-known. We do not pretend to have her love. If her brother were to come to harm because of something we allowed, how do you think she would react?"

It was a rhetorical question that didn't need answering. He knew exactly how Lyphnia would react, and he repressed a shiver. "You can tell her that I gave you no choice."

"Do you honestly think that would make a difference?" He stayed silent, and she took that as her answer. She shook her head, face suddenly crestfallen and sorrow in her voice. "We cannot risk everyone. If we keep him in good health, there is a chance that Regge's fever will pass. It is a slim chance, but still a chance."

"We have no choice." The Alpha whispered, wrapping an arm around his mate and pulling her to his side.

Rajiah bit the inside of his lip until he tasted blood on his tongue. It wasn't fair. He couldn't stand idly by while Regge fought for his life, not if there was something he could do about it. He understood their reasoning. He knew exactly what fate would befall them if a member of their pack were to give him the omega fever. Still, it was a difficult thing to swallow.

His hands curled into fists, nails biting into his palms. He turned his head to stare out over the mountains, in the direction of the valley. He could clear those tops easily, fly over them and straight for the valley. He could--

"No," he said suddenly, turning to face them once again. His voice must have been louder than intended because they all jumped and stared at him with wide eyes. "I'll go get help." Hope sparked in their faces. He was already pushing past them, heading for the open clearing. He tugged his shirt over his head, casting it to the ground. "I'll go and find a healer and bring one back." He shimmied out of his pants, kicking off his boots, and began pulling off the chains and bracelets and pendants that decorated his neck and wrists. He put them carefully atop the pile.

When he turned to glance over his shoulder, the entire pack was staring at him, faces a mixture of wariness and awe. The underlying buzz of excitement and hope was palatable.

He made eye contact with the Alpha, holding his gaze in a way that might have been threatening if the weretiger didn't know what his intentions were. "Keep him alive. I'll be back as soon as I can." And then he turned away, rolling his shoulders and feeling his muscles quiver and roll in anticipation.

He knelt, holding his arms up, head down, feeling the wave in his shoulder blades. They burned, itched, wings waiting and coiling beneath the surface, eager to sprout. He breathed deep, gathering in his strength, and tapped into that part of him that was always there, brimming beneath the surface. -- the pure, animalistic power. The air thickened around him, smoke leaking from his skin and curling around his flesh.

Then he threw his hands down as he leapt into the air with inhuman strength. He rose higher, the burn of the smoke and power ripping away at his flesh as his body expanded, and his scales rose to the surface. His wings burst forth, pumping downward powerfully to further propel him into the air. When his eyes snapped open, the world was bright and vivid and clear.

The smoke fled from his body, drifting and fading on the wind as his dragon form rose straight into the air. His wings pumped furiously to gain him altitude. And when he reached the height he wanted, he spread them out, catching the wind and leveling out his flight. The fading sunlight caught on his bronze scales, blazing brilliantly in warm colors.

He flew in one lazy circle above the tiger camp before shooting off in the direction of the valley.

He was small for his kind, but what he lacked in muscle mass and pure strength, he made up for in speed. His wings beat furiously, propelling him higher until he caught a favorable wind current, and still he beat them onward.

It had been ages since he had managed to fly like this, freely and quickly, pushing his limits and boundaries, without worries of being spotted by humans. The valley was too far from human civilization for that. Still, he wished the moment had come under better circumstances. Not when a young shifter's life was on the line.

Several hours later, moisture was crystalizing on his scales, his back muscles burned fiercely, and his lungs ached, but still he pushed onward. He was making good time. That much he knew. The valley, however, was still a pinprick in the distance. Night had fully fallen by then, the moon and the stars guiding his way. His enhanced eyesight let him see the mountain peaks that formed the valley, but he knew he was still a good distance away.

Grunting in frustration, he pushed himself harder, faster, further. He was close. And when he landed, he needed to find a healer, let them gather the necessary materials to battle the fever, and then—

Movement caught his eye.

He whipped his head around, trying to find it again. There. In the distance. A speck of shadow against the night sky. He narrowed his eyes, watching and waiting for the shape to once again obscure the stars. There. A massive, sleek shape with wings. It had to be a dragon. There was nothing else that would be out at this hour, flying this high.

A strange thrill went through him at the sight, as it did every time he saw another dragon. The excitement of seeing another of his kind, beautiful and powerful and rare, was followed closely by a sinking dread. He didn't exactly get along with most of his kin.

This dragon was a fair distance away from the valley, and it was flying in what appeared to be lazy circles, so it didn't look like a new arrival. Rather, it looked like someone out for a night flight.

Rajiah's first instinct was to ignore it, keep on his course, and hope the dragon wasn't curious enough to interfere, if it saw him at all. But... if that dragon was an alpha, or even a beta... and it was large with a wide wingspan that could carry them distances probably faster than Rajiah could...

His mind churned, thinking rapidly as he came to a decision: if he could enlist this dragon's help to go back to the tigers and then carry Regge to the valley, time would be saved. He wouldn't have to find a healer and wait for the healer to pack. And Regge wouldn't have to move after that.

His wings were already tipping in the wind, turning him in the other dragon's direction before he even realized he had made up his mind.

And once Rajiah made up his mind, he was set on his course. He was, after all, a dragon.

A wave of energy and determination crashing through him with renewed vigor, he shot off toward the other dragon, climbing higher and higher. When he was close, hovering at a higher altitude, he paused to get a good look at the other dragon. Giant. Black scales. Long, muscular body. Powerful wings with an impressive span. The wind brought to him the dragon's scent: male, strong, alpha. He was in a lazy, gliding flight, aimless and peaceful.He didn't give himself time to reconsider. Regge's life was on the line. He tucked his wings close to his body and went into a nosedive, angling directly for the other dragon. Rajiah's dive was sharp, fast, and precise. The dragon didn't whip his head around to stare until the very last moment. Rajiah unfolded his wings then, catching the wind and swooping up before impact. His upward swoop was short-lived as he tucked his wings again, twisting his body and dropping into a low loop around the other dragon, easily dodging around the other's wings and body.

As he came up on the other side, he paused, flapping his wings to tread air as their eyes met. The other dragon's eyes were as black as his scales, pools of shadow, glistening in the moonlight and fixed on him. His aura was stronger than Rajiah had anticipated, nearly choking him, easily pushing his own to the wayside and impressing on his will. And the strangest part? He didn't seem to be doing it purposefully.

He felt irritation, surprise, and curiosity flare in the alpha's aura, but Rajiah didn't stick around to see those come to fruition. He knew it was already enough to get the dragon's attention.

He flared his own aura, grinding his presence against the alpha's. He met the other dragon's eyes, refusing to budge or give way. He would not submit, and he made that clear. He also made it clear that he was not an omega looking for an alpha. This caused more curiosity to leak into the other man's aura.

Without warning, he twisted and dove away, flapping his wings furiously to gain distance. For good measure, as he turned, he made sure to lightly slap the alpha across the face with the tip of his tail, in an impolite but recognizable "follow me" gesture.

There was a pause and for a moment he was worried that the alpha wouldn't follow him. Then there was the sound of massive wings beating air, the rush of a body through the wind, a snarl of annoyance. Rajiah's heart hammered, wings pumping furiously to keep ahead of the alpha.

He was small and lithe and fast. But he was also tired from hours of flight and this alpha was bigger than most. In fact, he was the biggest dragon Rajiah had seen aside from the Elders. As such, he caught up easily.

Rajiah was forced to pull up abruptly as the larger dragon cut in front of him. Without missing a beat, he twisted and curved in the air, dodging around the other dragon and continuing onward. The black dragon gave chase. He kept trying to block Rajiah, and Rajiah kept twisting away. It made for an awkward dance in the sky, and Rajiah was getting frustrated. This was a waste of time, and Regge needed every minute. The alpha's aura kept pressing on him, kept urging him to submit. He snarled, pushing back.

The next time the black dragon went to block him, Rajiah growled and dove straight for the ground. His body was a bronze spear point, slick and fast as he shot toward the ground directly below them. He twisted his wings at the last moment, wings flaring out to slow his descent as smoke rose off his scales, dissolving his dragon body as he dropped the last short distance. When he landed, he was in human form again.

The night air was cool against his naked flesh, but it couldn't touch the fire inside him. He lifted his chin, amber eyes watching as the black dragon landed much more slowly. Black smoke whirled around his form as he came down, and the ground shook with the force of impact. When the air cleared, he stood up straight. He was tall, sleek black hair pushed away from his face. His body was built well, layers of toned muscles shifting and flexing beneath taut pale skin as he moved. Scars marred his flesh, but took away nothing from his dangerous beauty. His features were sharp, angular, and his dark, shadowed eyes stared holes into Rajiah's.

Rajiah shivered, but refused to cower. Neither of them moved. After hours of wind in his ears, the silence here was deafening. A calm breeze rolled past them, caressing his skin and ruffling his hair.

The alpha seemed content to stand and wait, pinning Rajiah with his gaze until he spoke first. Rajiah hated to give into him, but he didn't have time to play this power game.

"I need your help," he said, voice firm and loud enough to carry. He made it clear that he wasn't asking. He was demanding.

This seemed to take the alpha by surprise. He blinked several times, hard lines around his mouth and eyes relaxing a fraction. The pressure in his aura eased a little, just enough to let Rajiah know his guard was momentarily lowered. Rajiah pushed on.

"There's a tiger pack I've been traveling with." He pointed to the southeast. "A couple hours' flight that way. They're on their way to the valley, but they're still three-days' foot journey out. One of their pack, a young man, has the omega fever. He needs a healer now, or he might not survive the rest of the way." He couldn't help the way his expression scrunched up then, lip curling and nose wrinkling. "The pack leaders won't let me carry him to the valley in fear that I might contract the fever."

The man continued to stare, expression and body unmoving. The ends of his long, dark hair played in the breeze.

Rajiah's eyes narrowed, and he tried his best not to huff. "I need your help," he repeated, irritation entering his voice, impatience making itself known as he gestured again to the southeast. "A young boy is dying! I can't carry him to a healer, but you can!"

Silence. Impassive features. Cold, dark eyes.

"Hello?" He waved a hand in the air, trying to catch a flicker of movement, anything to indicate that the man was even alive. "Did you hear me?"

"Do you know who I am?" The question he had heard hundreds of times before from countless men and women, both dragon and not. It was a question that was usually said with haughty arrogance, spoken in disbelief. But the alpha's voice was soft, surprised, honestly curious. There was the question there, yes, but it wasn't spoken in self-importance. It was as if he honestly found it hard to believe that Rajiah didn't know who he was.

Irritation overcame him. "Does it matter?" Silence again. Rajiah groaned, throwing his hands up in the air. "We're wasting time!"

"Why should I help?"

"What?"

"Why should I help?" Again, his voice was filled with so much soft surprise, so much honest curiosity, that Rajiah found himself gaping. He sounded like a child questioning things that should be obvious. Yet he stood solid and firm as a man, a slash of pale flesh and dark shadows in the night. "I don't know this boy or his pack. What reason do I have to help?"

Anger, sharp and hot, boiled in Rajiah's blood. He stomped forward, closing the distance between them swiftly. The other weredragon was taller than he was, but Rajiah didn't feel small when he had to tilt his head back to meet the alpha's gaze. Ignoring the strong aura, he jabbed the man in the chest with a finger. "Because you can. Because he is young and has a life to live. Because he is a shifter. He may not be a dragon, but he is one of our own. If we don't look after those weaker than us, then what good are we?"

He hadn't meant to shout, yet here he was, shouting at an alpha and jabbing his chest so hard the man stumbled back a step. He stared down at Rajiah's blazing gaze, dark eyes wide in surprise. His lips were relaxed, parting just slightly as he gaped. Silent. Still.

"I don't have time for this," Rajiah huffed, turning on his heel and stalking away so he had enough space to shift and take flight again. "Regge doesn't have time for this." He gathered his strength, reaching for his inner dragon, feeling the heat of his scales close to the surface--

"Wait," The voice spoke without urgency, without rush, not shouted and not yelled. But it was a demand that stopped Rajiah in his tracks, keeping his feet on the ground. He turned slowly, eyeing the alpha cautiously. He seemed to have recovered from his surprise and stood tall and firm, as expressionless as ever. "I will help."

Rajiah's heart skipped a beat. "Really?" he breathed, searching the alpha's face.

He nodded once. "Lead me to the boy. I'll get him to the valley."

Rajiah's heart pounded, hope burning in his veins. He nodded, lips tilting into a small smile. "Thank you. Follow me."

He took several running steps, leaping into the air and shifting with ease, feeling the burning of his bones, the ripping of his muscles, the smoke that whirled as his flesh burned to cinder and his scales rose to the surface. He took to the sky, wings pumping as adrenaline sang through his body. The black dragon rose behind him, slower at first but easily closing the distance. Rajiah steered their course to the southeast, pushing his body as hard and as fast as he could go.

They made it to the tiger camp before sunrise. Rajiah landed like a meteor crashing to the surface, leaving a small crater in his wake from the force of the impact. As soon as his feet were under him, he was running into the camp, to where the pack gathered. Their eyes weren't on him; however, they were gazing at the black dragon circling above.

"Is he still alive?"

"Yes," the weretiger Alpha said, awe and distraction in his voice. "Who is—"

"I found someone on my way to the valley. He's an alpha, so he can't catch the fever, and with his wingspan he can fly faster than I can... He's going to take Regge to the valley."

"Rajiah, are you sure--"

"We can trust him," he said with certainty. He may not know the dragon, but a dragon was true to his word. The earth shook as the black dragon landed, standing in human form and striding to where Rajiah stood. He waved a hand as the man stopped next to him. "This is..." He trailed off, expression twisting in uncertainty. He glanced sideways, brow furrowed and lips pursed in a small frown. "What is your name?"

The man glanced at him then, eyebrows raised, dark eyes oddly amused and relaxed. And then something strange happened with his features: he smiled. It was small, the barest tilt to his lips, a little lopsided in nature, almost like a smirk, confident and at ease. This close, and with the firelight from the pack's camp, Rajiah could see the man's human features clearly for the first time. There was something familiar about the sharpness of his nose, the high cheekbones, the crinkle at the edges of eyes like dark pools, the way his thin lips cocked just so... Rajiah couldn't put his finger on it. Recognition nagged at the edges of his memory, picking and prodding at a wall it couldn't quite break through. Rajiah had been alive for centuries, and he had met many dragons. The odds of having met this one were very high.

And when the man spoke, his voice was even and unhurried, edges laced with an innate authority but softened by what

Rajiah thought might have been amusement. "Arulean Black."

Recognition flared through him, crashing through that wall in his mind and flooding his memory: a tall man, cocky and sure, a smirk constantly on his lips, confidence and ease in his manner, grace in his step, discharging power and authority with every gesture. A man, a king, kind and handsome, ruthless and arrogant, a large black dragon twisting across the sky with the scarlet form of Lyphnia at his side.

Rajiah's eyes widened, and his jaw went slack, lips parting as he gaped. The man's smirk curled just a hair wider, something dancing in those dark eyes. Yes, he was definitely amused.

He turned away from Rajiah to the tigers, who were just as astounded as Rajiah was. They stood frozen, eyes flickering from Arulean to their Alpha. After a moment of tense silence, the Alpha of the weretiger pack fell to his knees. "My lord..." he said gruffly, and seconds later the rest of the pack followed suit.

Rajiah remained where he stood, at a loss for words.

Arulean held up a hand, cutting off whatever the Alpha was going to say. "Please, rise. From what I've been told, the young shifter does not have much time."

The words snapped Rajiah out of his stupor. "It's urgent," Rajiah affirmed, stepping forward to head for the tent. "This way."

Arulean followed him, and the weretigers parted, closing in the gap as they passed. Rajiah waited outside the tent as Arulean ducked inside. He crossed his arms over his chest, tapping his foot impatiently as he waited, straining to hear the murmured words between Arulean and Regge's mother. He reemerged moments later, Regge wrapped in a blanket and looking small cradled against the big man's chest.

The Alpha dragon paused as he passed Rajiah. "I'll take him to the castle's healer. He'll be well cared for. Make sure the pack gets to the valley and escort the child's family to the castle when they arrive."

Rajiah didn't like taking orders, but he nodded...

Arulean handed Regge to the pack's Alpha before stepping forward into the open space. The tiger pack shuffled back to give him room as he shifted into his dragon form. Looking at him now, with his massive size and jet-black scales, Rajiah felt foolish for not recognizing him. Arulean Black was renowned throughout the shifter world. He had been a dragon king, one who had been at the forefront of the war during the Purge. He was mated to Rajiah's sister. Still, Rajiah hadn't been thinking about that. He had been only thinking of getting help. He hadn't expected the dragon king to be so far from his kingdom during the dead of night.

Once shifted, Arulean took the bundled Regge in his front claws, the layers of blankets cushioning his body and providing warmth for when they reached higher altitudes. Arulean spread his wings high, preparing for flight, and then paused. His dark eyes moved over the pack until they focused on Rajiah, and he shivered.

"Be swift" he found himself saying, knowing the dragon would hear him.

There was a barely perceptible nod and then came the powerful downbeat of his wings. Arulean took to the sky with a speed and grace that defied his size. He circled the camp once, caught the wind, and shot out toward the northwest. Rajiah watched him go until his scales could no longer be seen against the night sky.

He felt foolish for not recognizing the dragon king, but took amused comfort in the fact that the man hadn't recognized him either.

CHAPTER

THREE

Weeks after the summoning, dragons started to trickle into the valley. The Summit was traditionally held on the first full moon after the summoning in order to give everyone plenty of time to arrive. They came at all hours of the day and night, circling the valley before landing on the flight grounds below the castle. Their first stop was always to pay respect to Arulean and Lyphnia and to officially announce their presence.

The two of them were always ready. It was easy to feel a dragon's presence long before it arrived, and if they weren't paying attention, they had scouts to alert them. While that dragon circled the valley, Arulean and Lyphnia would shuffle to the great hall to await the new arrival. They would stand regal and proud on the dais in front of their thrones. They would gracefully accept any gift or well wishes the dragon had brought, and then they'd ask a servant to show the guest to a room. The castle had hundreds of guest rooms to accommodate their kin. They even had more cave-like rooms deep in the mountain side for those who felt more comfortable there.

Then with the formalities dispensed with, the two of them would go their separate ways, as they did every day. He wouldn't see Lyphnia again until the next guest arrived, and he wouldn't actively seek her out. He was certain that since the summoning, this was the most he had seen her in years. They usually went days or even weeks without seeing each other, even though they both lived in the castle.

"Disappointed yet again?" Lyphnia said as their latest guest was escorted out of the great hall, leaving the two of them alone. There was a teasing lilt to her voice, one that Arulean did not like.

"What reason do I have to be disappointed?" He asked, voice even and almost bored as he picked at a loose thread on his sleeve. He took the steps slowly down from the dais. The click of her heels was right behind him.

"Arulean, don't play games. I've known you far too long for that. I can read you better than you care to admit."

In that, she was unfortunately right. He was disappointed, but that wasn't a fact he wanted to disclose to her, and it unnerved him greatly that she could pick up that much. "I have no idea what you mean, my dear."

He clasped his hands behind his back, chin held high and expression neutral as he strode almost lazily across the great hall. She kept pace with him, examining her nails. "If I didn't know better, I would say you're waiting for a specific person." Years of concealing his own thoughts kept him from flinching. He saw her eye him sideways, looking for a crack in his armor. He showed her none.

"What gives you that idea?" He let hints of false amusement leak into his voice, trying to make it sound like an absurd idea.

Judging from her slight frown, it worked. "You seem almost excited whenever we're about to greet a guest. And I do say 'almost' in the barest of terms, but when you haven't shown excitement in decades, just a little goes a long way. However, your excitement fades whenever we see our new arrival."

He shrugged, melancholy etched into his features and weighing heavily on his shoulders. "It's always a pleasure to see familiar faces, especially when we go decades without seeing them. But the faces I see are no longer familiar." Their faces were lined with weariness, bitterness, a hopelessness that couldn't be ignored but was far too recognizable. They were no longer lively, strong, or proud. Even the most boisterous dragons held an edge of fragility about them that threatened to shatter. Their race was not as it once had been, and that was a sorrow that ate away at his heart. The face of every dragon he saw was a grim reminder of the current state of things. The nostalgia that every guest brought was no longer sweet, but tainted and sour. "Our numbers are dwindling, and it is at times like these when that is seen all too clearly."

They paused in the hallway outside the great hall, turning to face each other. Her lips were pursed, face lined with thoughts he couldn't read. She used to be so open to him. He used to know her as well as he knew himself. But those days were gone. She, too, was a stranger to him. "Something needs to be done."

He regarded her, answering as neutrally as he could. "Agreed. Something must be done." He knew, however, that their opinions on the matter differed greatly. And that was an argument he was not willing to have again. Not here. Not now. He bowed gracefully. "If you'll excuse me, my dear. I have matters that need attending to."

Her smile was wry and her voice amused, the pleasant sound of her voice clipped and cold at the edges. "Don't you always."

They went their separate ways, and it wasn't until he could no longer feel her oppressive aura pressing against his that he felt like he could finally breathe again. Truth be told, Lyphnia was right. And he hated that she was right.

It had been three days, and he had yet to see the young omega dragon he had left with the weretigers. They should be arriving today, which meant the dragon would have to make his appearance at the castle first and foremost. But Arulean found himself thinking of the stubborn fire in those amber eyes, the way he didn't quake under the pressure of Arulean's aura, and he found himself wondering if the omega would even come to the castle at all.

But no, he had to. The young tiger was still here, in the infirmary.

Arulean found himself pausing at a hall juncture. It was a rare enough thing that he surprised himself. He'd lived in this castle for centuries. He had helped to plan and build it. He knew these halls like the back of his hand. He walked through them with purpose. He always knew exactly where he wanted to go and how to get there, steps never faltering or stopping in their journey. And yet here he paused, here his feet read his mind before even he did, sensing his hesitation. He never second-guessed his destination, yet now, he was.

His eyes drifted down a hallway. The infirmary was in that direction. He knew the young tiger would survive the fever. Arulean had specifically asked to be kept informed of his condition. He hadn't, however, visited since dropping him off three days ago. He idly wondered if he should. Regge, he remembered. Regge was his name. Yet, he still didn't know the name of the dragon shifter who had bullied him out of the sky to ask for a favor.

If we don't look after those weaker than us, then what good are we?

The words still remained with him, repeating in his mind like a mantra, intruding whenever his mind went quiet, haunting him when he tried to sleep, to focus. As much as he was loathe to admit it, he was eager to meet the young dragon again. It was a strange thing. He hadn't felt this kind of anticipation or excitement in years. Anticipation was always soured by dread or apprehension, never light-hearted and almost giddy with an innocent interest. It made him feel young again, and that was an odd feeling.

He hadn't even gotten the dragon's name. And while he looked familiar, as almost all dragon kin did at this point, he couldn't put a name to the omega's face. He'd met so many dragons throughout his long life. It was hard to keep track of who was alive and who had died. And this omega was younger than most. Arulean doubted he had fought in the wars. He couldn't shake the eerie familiarity that niggled at the edges of his mind, but out of his reach. He felt haunted by the fire in those gorgeous amber eyes, by the determined lines of his face, by the shadow of a smile that he had managed to glimpse. The subtleties of his scent ghosting through his memory added to the sensation that he was missing something. His scent was so subtle that Arulean had at first mistaken him for a beta.

Needless to say, there were many things about the young dragon that intrigued Arulean, and he was eager to meet him again under proper circumstances. He wanted to see him, to know what kind of man would talk to him with blatant disrespect, without fear, and leave him with words that haunted him for days after their meeting. Words that made him question himself. Words that made his steps pause in the halls he had known for centuries.

He wanted to know who he was so the mystery could be put to rest. Perhaps then he could move on to more important matters.

He continued toward the stairs and climbed up to his study.

Focus, he found, was hard to come by. The castle and the valley were anything but peaceful. If the flashing of dragon auras everywhere wasn't distracting enough, it was the sound of constant movement throughout the castle. Even the village in the valley below buzzed with energy.

He stared at his ledgers and papers and journals, tapping the tip of his quill against the worn wood of his desk. His chin rested in his palm, eyes turned toward the open doors and fluttering curtains. Sighing, he gave into temptation and stood, striding out onto the balcony. He rested his hands on the smooth stone of the railing, letting his gaze sweep out across the valley. It had once been just a small village beneath their castle, and had rapidly grown throughout the centuries as more and more shifters migrated to them, hoping to live safely beneath the dragons' watchful gaze and away from humans.

If we don't look after those weaker than us, then what good are we?

Perhaps he had already been abiding by that philosophy without realizing it. He had always had a soft spot for shifters, but he had always seen the lesser ones as just that: lesser. They were nothing compared to his own kind, and regarded them as barely more than humans. Still, they were respectful and bowed to him, so he let them stay. Dragons were prone to pride and vanity. He was no different. Having a village of worshippers on his front doorstep he had seemed like god. As the war went on and the Purge worsened, more and more filtered in, looking for a haven. He had let them in, despite Lyphnia's sneers and disdainful looks.

Without realizing it, he had created a safe haven for shifters of all breeds.

His fingers tapped the stone, eyes surging upward and searching the horizon. He spotted a few scales reflecting the late afternoon sun, but they were all dragons who had already arrived. He had committed each of them to memory: faces, names, auras, scales. Each of them was catalogued in his mind and in a book in his study. A list of the rare, the magnificent, the dying. Each name should be a reason to rejoice, but instead all he could think of was how a thousand years ago, there would have been too many to remember them all.

Something had to be done.

A knock at his study doors brought him out of his thoughts. He half-turned as the heavy oaken doors were hesitantly pushed open and a servant poked her head in. A wolf, by the scent of her. She searched the study, eyes wary. "My lord?"

"Here." He said, voice loud enough to carry.

She jumped, eyes finding him before lowering respectfully. She stepped fully into the room, curtseying before clasping her hands in front of her. "The queen has requested your presence."

He raised an eyebrow, face otherwise unmoving. "Has she now?" He asked dryly. The maid blanched, and he sighed inwardly. When he spoke again, he softened his tone. The sharpness hadn't been for her, but for his mate. She was merely a messenger. "What does the queen need me for?" It was rare for her to summon him at all. When she did, she made sure to let him know she wanted him to go to her. She never sought him out herself unless she was particularly impatient.

"I believe the queen's brother has arrived. The one escorting the Great Mother's ashes."

Arulean felt his brows pinch together just a fraction. "I did not feel the presence of a new dragon entering the valley." He would have felt him. A dragon's aura was stronger in their beast form. He would have felt him as he flew over the mountains, a new speck in the rainbow collage of draconic presences in the valley.

The maid fidgeted, eyes darting to him and then down to the floor. "I only know what the queen told me ..."

He sighed. Of course, the woman wouldn't have answers for him. "Thank you. Do you know where I might find the queen?"

The maid seemed to fidget just a little more. When she spoke, her words were chosen carefully. "When I left her, the queen was in the entry hall..."

He sighed again.. "She just said that I would find her, did she not?" The maid nodded. "I suppose I should do that. Thank you." He waved a hand to dismiss her, and she curtseyed again before slipping out the door.

He heaved a heavy sigh and strode back to his desk, closing his books and journals and putting his quill away. He carried out each action slowly, with extreme care and precision, and when he headed for the door, each step was slow and deliberate. If Lyphnia wanted to play a power game in making him find her, then he would do the same and make her wait.

His study was on one of the upper floors of the castle, and he headed for the grand staircase that led down through the heart of the building. Each step was careful and slow, hands clasped behind his back, chin held high. He walked as if he was out for a stroll without a care in the world, and not as though he was looking for his mate.

While he walked, he mentally searched for her. She wasn't hard to find. Her aura was as bright and red and fiery as her scales, as dark and writhing as the red depths of her eyes. She burned brightly, a comet moving throughout the castle and the valley at all hours of the day. He knew his own was like a cloud, a void, smoke, a shadow, oppressive and dark. Fire and ice. Two opposing forces that ruled the valley and held power above dragons. Two clashing forces that were at, what felt like an eternal stalemate.

Any dragon would be able to find either of them easily, just as he found Lyphnia. She was walking along one of the halls on the lower levels of the castle, not too far from the great hall. There was a small aura that burned dimly beside hers, but it was easily overpowered and hidden by her own. He had no doubt that was her brother.

As a child of the Great Mother, Lyphnia had many siblings. She was not the oldest nor the youngest by far, but was perhaps the strongest and the most well-known. She took after her mother in that way. Most of her siblings, however, were no longer alive. Many of them had sided with her during the wars and the Purge, and, as such, she led them to their untimely doom. He would be foolish to believe none of them were left. The Great Mother had continued to give birth long after the Purge, but there must be something special about this one. From what Arulean had gathered, he was the only child present at the time of their Mother's passing, hence he was tasked with carrying her ashes to the burial chamber. A heavy but important responsibility that no one took lightly, which made it even stranger that Arulean hadn't felt the dragon's presence as the latter entered the valley.

For a moment, he entertained the idea that the dragon might be a submissive one, with a faint aura that was easily hidden by those around him, much like he was by Lyphnia now. And then with a dry humored scoff, Arulean dismissed the idea. If he was indeed a child of the Great Mother and a brother to Lyphnia, Arulean had no reason to believe he would be submissive. Their line had a fire in them that kept them pushing forward, for better or worse.

As with most of dragon-kind, he couldn't remember most of Lyphnia's siblings. He remembered some of them, but most were gone. And of the ones whom he knew were alive, he couldn't think of one that would have been there at the time of their mother's death. They were all far too stubborn and independent to stay around each other for long.

He wasn't sure what to expect from this brother, but he steeled himself for the worst. If he was anything like Lyphnia, which they tended to be, then Arulean would have his hands full. She didn't need another hot-headed dragon in her corner. There were plenty already.

He steered his path to intercept them, leisurely strolling down the intricate and well decorated halls of his home. He heard her voice before he saw them. It wasn't the cold, biting tone she used with him, but it wasn't warm and inviting either. It was her queenly voice with a touch of familiarity as she told her brother about the castle and the things they passed: paintings, sculptures, rugs, tapestries. There wasn't any response, but he knew she didn't need one.

He braced himself, locking his expression carefully neutral as he rounded a corner and into view.

"Ah, Arulean! There you are," she said, gesturing to him and speaking as if they had been looking for him, which they hadn't, or waiting on him, which was likely. Her smile was fixed in place, a smile she knew how to craft and make look genuine. "My dear, come say hello to our newest guest." She waved him forward, but he didn't pick up his pace, only stopping when they were several feet away. He held her gaze, letting her silently know that he was displeased with her method of summoning him. If anything, her smile curled more widely.

"This is my younger brother, Rajiah Bronze."

Arulean's gaze slid to the young man, and his breath caught in his throat.

He was shorter than Lyphnia, but not by much. With his lithe build, he had a body humans might mistake for weak. But Arulean knew better. He knew the strength dragons possessed. He could see it in the finely defined muscles of his exposed forearms, in the way he held himself. His skin was light brown, warm and inviting. His hair was a thick mass of dark waves that brushed his shoulders, tucked behind his ears. He was dressed simply: a tunic that wrapped around his torso with short sleeves, a scarf-like strip of cloth wrapped around his waist, and somewhat loose pants tucked into the tops of his boots. The colors were all in browns and dark reds. His wrists were adorned with thick gold bands and bracelets, matching those around his slender neck.

His most striking feature, however, was his eyes. Dark amber blazing with a fire from within, meeting his steadily, amusement dancing in their depths. The corners of his full lips were curved up just slightly, completing the look of mischief that seemed to cling to him like a second skin.

He was beautiful, which wasn't too surprising. He was related to Lyphnia and the Great Mother, after all. And all dragons possessed an unearthly beauty. More importantly, he was the dragon shifter who had the brash courage to near attack a dragon king and coerce him out of the sky to ask a favor.

Rajiah Bronze. A name to remember for sure.

Arulean recovered from his surprise quickly. "I did not feel you fly in," he found himself saying.

Lyphnia answered for him, waving a hand in dismissal. "He walked into the valley. Can you imagine? Said he traveled with a pack of weretigers." She ruffled his hair in a gesture that might have been affectionate and perhaps a little amused. "And with mother's ashes in tow. She would have your hide if she knew."

"Then it's a good thing she's gone and has no say in the matter," Rajiah said calmly, eyes never leaving Arulean's.

She scoffed, good natured, crossing her arms over her chest and cocking a hip to the side. "Remind me to never let you carry my ashes."

He doubted Lyphnia would need that assistance anytime soon. She was far too stubborn to die.

He took a step forward, taking the young dragon's hand in his own and having the pleasure of seeing the amusement fade from his lips. He bowed over his hand, toying with the idea of pressing his lips to it before tossing it away. "It is a pleasure to formally meet you, Rajiah," he said, ever graceful and elegant. He glanced up at the young man, feeling one corner of his lips twitch into a small, smug smirk as a light flush darkened the omega's cheeks.

Lyphnia raised an eyebrow, good humor gone as she observed them. "You two have met recently?" She asked, voice carefully even, curious.

Arulean straightened, dropping Rajiah's hand as he turned to look at his mate. He raised one of his own eyebrows. "Recently? Have we met previously?"

Lyphnia put a hand on Rajiah's shoulder, shifting closer to him in a clear possessive gesture. Her kin, her family. Not his. It didn't escape Arulean that the young dragon shifted just an inch away. "Rajiah came here shortly after he presented, at our mother's request. We attempted to find him a mate, but... he was stubborn."

Both of Arulean's eyebrows rose at that, and he looked back and forth between them. In truth, they looked very little alike. He knew that Lyphnia took after her mother, but the only similarities between them were their delicate, upturned noses and their eyes, dark with shifting glints of blazing color. The Great Mother was known to have had many mates, and most of her children were only half-siblings. He was willing to bet Rajiah took after his father.

"Is that so?" Arulean asked, allowing his surprise to show. He wracked his brain, rummaging through centuries' worth of memories, but couldn't pinpoint Rajiah's face in any of them. His eyes settled on the omega as he asked as casually as he could, "And have you found a mate since?" He ignored the strange, dark feeling coiling low in his gut.

"No," Rajiah said, familiar stubbornness lining his face. "I still haven't." He said it like a challenge, like he was daring Arulean to question him, to look down on him for being unattached as an omega.

The dark, sickening feeling loosened, and Arulean said nothing more on the matter.

That, however, didn't stop Lyphnia from saying, "Much to

mother's dismay. She tried for centuries to find Rajiah a mate."

"No one has appealed to me."

"That's not the point." She said sharply, turning her narrowed gaze on him. Rajiah met it without flinching, his own aura flaring beside hers. Ah, yes, Arulean could see how they were related. "You are an omega—"

"And I won't settle for an alpha purely for the purpose of procreating."

The tension was thick enough to be tangible. Arulean noticed several servants step into the hall only to turn heel and walk away. Even the lowest of shifters could feel the pressing auras of two dragons in an argument.

"Perhaps now is not the time to discuss these matters," Arulean said diplomatically, with an edge of authority that made people listen.

Lyphnia tore her gaze from her brother, lips pursing as she looked him over. "Perhaps you're right," she conceded, before looking between them. "So if you do not remember meeting him centuries ago, how do you know each other?"

Arulean nodded at Rajiah, clasping his hands behind his back. "He found me in flight three days ago and asked if I would bring a sick weretiger to a healer."

"Ah," Her eyes lit up with understanding, her gaze shifting to her brother. "So you're the reason there's a tiger in my infirmary." Her voice was almost admonishing, as though he was a child who had been caught red-handed, and not an adult who had begged Arulean to save a life.

Rajiah didn't look at her. Instead his eyes were on Arulean as he gave a small half-bow. "Thank you for helping him. How is he?"

"I've been told that he is in good health. His fever broke and he is well on his way to recovery."

Rajiah smiled then. A small smile, barely there but incredibly genuine. Something in Arulean shifted at the sight of it. "I'm glad to hear that." He turned to his sister. "Where is the infirmary?"

She frowned, plump red lips pursing as her brows furrowed. "You need to carry mother's ashes to the burial chamber."

His hands automatically went to a sash of cloth tied diagonally across his chest, shifting the bag slung across his back that Arulean hadn't noticed before. No doubt it held the urn of the Great Mother. "She can wait. There's no rush."

Lyphnia's frown deepened. "You have a duty."

"And I'll do it. After I make sure Regge is alright and let him know his family is in the valley."

They locked eyes for a long, tense moment, and Arulean wondered if he'd have to break up another squabble before it started. But Lyphnia looked away, shrugging and waving a hand. "Do as you like. Mother isn't around anymore to complain." She turned on her heel and strode away without any formal gesture of goodbye. "I'm going for a flight. You can find me when you're ready to go to the burial chamber. Ask a servant to take you to the infirmary."

They watched her go, steps quick and staccato with purpose. She didn't once look back, nor did she bid either of them farewell. Arulean was far too used to this behavior to feel ruffled by it.

"I can take you there." Arulean said, breaking the silence.

Rajiah looked at him then, surprise and suspicion clear on his face. "I can find a servant if you're busy."

Arulean shook his head, turning on his heel and gesturing for Rajiah to follow. "Nonsense. I know the way." He wanted to say that he had nothing better to do, but he knew that would be a lie.

They walked the halls in silence, Rajiah at his side but trailing a fraction behind. The infirmary was on the far wing of the castle, and it gave them some time.

"I trust the rest of the pack arrived safely?" Arulean asked idly.

Rajiah eyed him sidelong, but nodded. "Yes, they've taken up temporary residence in one of the inns in the valley. They plan on coming tomorrow to pay their respects and pay tribute to you for helping them."

Arulean shook his head. "They need not give anything."

"You went out of your way to help them." Rajiah protested, brows furrowing.

Arulean glanced sideways at him, corners of his lips curling. "Weren't you the one who told me it was my duty to look after those weaker than us?"

Rajiah opened his mouth to respond, then snapped it shut. He turned to face forward, lips pressed together and cheeks flushed. Arulean felt his smile widen. "They would still like to thank you," he grumbled. "It would be disrespectful to refuse."

Arulean nodded. He understood that much. "Fine, but I leave it to you to make sure they don't give anything of value." He opened his mouth to protest, but Arulean held up a hand to cut him off. "They may bring a gift of thanks, if that is their wish, but make sure it is nothing of value. They have so little as it is, and they mean to start a new life here. I have enough."

Rajiah was silent for a moment before he muttered a soft, "All right." There was something surprised there, something kind, something warm. Arulean risked a glance and knew he shouldn't have the moment he saw that tender smile. He looked away.

"Your sister was not happy I brought a weretiger to our castle's healer."

"I'm not surprised. But she didn't force him to leave, and that's what matters."

"Of course, she didn't. I insisted he stay here." He said, idly shrugging one shoulder. "She may have power here, but I have more. She picks her battles carefully, and this was not one she wanted to fight."

There was a pause, and then a curious and carefully neutral, "Do the two of you fight often?"

Arulean couldn't help it. He laughed. It was a soft chuckle, bubbling up and out of his throat without his permission, catching him off guard. It wasn't a boisterous laugh, but it was more than he had done in years. It was the absurdity of the question that had caught him off guard, sparking his dry amusement. Anyone who had been anywhere near the valley in the past millennia knew that he and Lyphnia fought often. They rarely ever saw eye-to-eye, even before the Purge. There had just been a passion in their youth that had covered that up, kept things mild, and allowed them to look past their differences. With that passion gone, all that was left was a healthy understanding and respect for each other's bound-aries and their silent stalemate.

"That is putting it mildly," he said when his laughter subsided, lips curled in a smile. Rajiah said nothing, and moments later, he stopped next to an open doorway. "The infirmary is through here."

He stayed in the doorway, leaning against the frame with his arms crossed over his chest as he silently watched Rajiah reunite with Regge. He observed the instant relief in Rajiah, relaxing his whole body and showing easy smiles, a warm laugh, and kind eyes. Something inside Arulean stirred again. Something he was afraid to name.

Rajiah Bronze. A name to remember indeed.

CHAPTER
FOUR

At his sister's insistence, he flew to the burial chamber with his mother's urn wrapped up tightly and clutched in his claws. It had been a while since they had flown. Hell, it had been centuries since he had seen her. She was the most well-known of his siblings, and arguably the most powerful. Everything about her exuded strength, cunning, and a crafty authority that had snared her one of the more suitable mates among dragon-kind and a title of queen.

Her dragon form was larger than his, but not by much. They were built similar in stature: lithe, slim and lean. Built for speed and aerial maneuvering rather than sheer power in flight. Her scales were a beautiful, deep red, horns slim and sharp. The spines on her back were dark as her eyes, wings gracefully curved. She flew with a grace that was unparalleled, rolling through the wind as if it were made to be her servant.

It was little wonder Arulean fell for her, he thought with a bitterness that surprised him.

He let Lyphnia lead him, though he knew where they were going. She flew lazy circles around him, twisting him in the air and playfully batting at his wings and tail with hers. He nipped at her, and she shoved into him. Once, when he was small, little more than a hatchling, she had flown with him like this. Playful and teasing, light and content, without a care in the world. That was a long time ago. Even now, there was an edge of authority, of power mongering in her actions. Little subtle hints and clues behind her movements, in the way she held herself, that told him that she clearly was setting herself above him. Once upon a time, she had not needed to resort to petty displays of authority to assert her dominance.

They landed at the bottom of the steps outside the cave on light feet, smoke peeling off their skin and dissipating into the chilly mountain air. The wind nipped at their exposed flesh, causing goosebumps to rise. Neither of them were bothered by it, however. They were dragons, and their internal temperature ran hot. With the wrapped urn cradled in his arms, the two of them climbed the steps at an unhurried pace.

The keeper was waiting for them at the top, just outside the mouth of the cave. His hands were clasped in front of him, the hood of his robe pulled up over his head. His expression was blank and neutral, but in a way that spoke of contentment and peace. Unlike Arulean's near constant neutral state, which spoke of ice storms and a cold heart.

As they reached the top of the steps, the keeper bowed. "My lady," he said politely to Lyphnia before turning to Rajiah. "My lord."

Rajiah shook his head, lips curling in distaste but speaking with good humor when he said, "Please, Rajiah is just fine."

The man's lips quirked, eyes dancing with a shared amusement. "Rajiah, then. Welcome." He made a gesture, and two acolytes, dressed in similar robes with far less embroidery, stepped forward, each of them offering a robe to Rajiah and Lyphnia. She held out her arms for the acolyte to dress her, barely looking at the shifter. Rajiah was more accommodating, muttering a soft thanks and offering a smile.

The keeper led them into the cave and through the maze of tunnels, lit by torches and glow stone, to the burial chamber.

Rajiah had to stop just inside, mouth falling open in awe. He had never been in here. He'd never had reason to. It was a very sacred place, hidden deep within the mountain. Few dragons were allowed inside. Few wanted to enter at all, and Rajiah could understand why.

The whole cavern, massive and empty and echoing, vibrated with a foreign energy, the remnants of the auras of hundreds of dragons long since passed. He could feel their presence humming around him, shaking him down to his bones, setting his teeth on edge and making his hair stand on end. He felt like he could hear the ghost of whispers, unclear and near silent, speaking to him just outside of his hearing, making him question whether he heard them at all. It felt like the shadows of fingers were caressing his skin, touches light and airy with a strange sense of awe and desperation.

Lyphnia glanced back at him, noting his pause with a raised brow and a quirked lip. "You get used to it."

He shook himself, body wracked in an involuntary shiver before hurrying to catch up to her side. "I don't see how..." He muttered, glancing around. The ceiling was too high to see, and the cavern walls were dotted and marred with shadows and hidden alcoves.

She shrugged. "They can't hurt you. Arulean says they feel lonely. I don't think they feel anything. It's just energy."

Rajiah tried to suppress his unease. Energy or not, it was a solemn place. The keeper led them to the lodestone at the center before stopping and turning to face them. He held out his hands expectantly, and Rajiah unwrapped the stone urn before handing it over. The keeper took it carefully and reverently with a small, half-bow.

Rajiah and Lyphnia stepped back as the acolytes stepped

from the shadows, melting away like ghosts. Lyphnia's face was fixed in a sneer at the sight of them, but she kept her words to herself. They watched in silence as they gathered around the lodestone and began chanting in the language of the ancients. The Mother Tongue, nearly forgotten, still beating in the hearts of dragons, power dripping from every word.

The tattoos adorning their skin began to glow as they chanted, and the lodestone hummed with power. With a flick of his wrist, the keeper tossed a handful of their mother's ashes into the air, watching them float down to land on the stone. The energy humming in the room seemed to increase, pressing on them from all sides, oddly familiar and, yet, entirely foreign. He found it hard to breathe, and started taking more steps back. He felt like he was intruding, and the strangeness of the cavern was quickly becoming too much.

It wasn't much longer before he muttered an excuse and slipped outside. He found his way through the maze of tunnels by following the smell of fresh air. Once outside, he closed his eyes, breathing deeply and letting the chilly air burn his lungs and cleanse his senses, and bring with it a calmer clarity.

The burial chamber was a sacred place, but it wasn't heavily guarded. He now understood why. Despite how much power could be wielded in there, he didn't know any dragon who would be foolish enough to try. He imagined their ancestors, even from the afterlife, would rebel should a lesser dragon attempt to use the lodestone. He was almost surprised Arulean and Lyphnia were able to do it.

Then again, they were both incredible dragons with plenty of power of their own.

"I don't know how you can stand to be in there," he said as he felt Lyphnia walk up beside him.

"As I said, you get used to it. It's easier if you remember they're only the leftover energies of our kind. The fact remains that they're dead, and they can't do anything to harm us. They cannot affect us, but we can use them."

"Do you ever feel specific auras?" he asked, voice soft. "Specific people buried there?"

"I try not to." She almost sounded sad.

Rajiah hummed his acknowledgement, and the two of them stood in a comfortable silence, wind playing with the loose edges of their robes and tugging at their hair. The mountain was the highest peak in the area, and the mouth of the cave towered over many of the surrounding mountains. The valley could be seen as a dip and speck in the distance. Close enough to be near, but far enough away that the burial chamber felt remote.

He was a little disappointed that Arulean hadn't joined them, but he couldn't say he was surprised, not after feeling the tension between him and Lyphnia. It was such an odd contrast from the last time he had seen them. When he visited centuries ago, before the Purge, when they were still young and very much attached, their auras hadn't clashed as they did now. They had seemed to reach for each other, intertwining in a supernova that was hard to ignore. It forced dragons to their knees in submission, which was no doubt how they had been given the titles of king and queen. Their eyes had always searched for one another, with a primal hunger and passion that had made Rajiah turn away.

There was no trace of that left, and it was a jarring comparison. Rajiah could still hear Arulean's hollow laugh when he'd asked if they often fought, and could still see the cold sneer with which Lyphnia regarded her mate.

Dragons had long lifespans, but he had never witnessed mates becoming so cold to one another to such a drastic extent.

"How was she?" Lyphnia asked, breaking the silence and drawing him out of his thoughts. He glanced sideways at her, admiring her powerful and beautiful profile as she stood, back straight and chin high, arms crossed over her chest. "In her last moments," she continued. "How was she?"

Rajiah looked away, eyes fixing over the horizon and the rolling mountain peaks. "The same as she was in life." He heard Lyphnia's soft, amused snort, and found himself smiling wryly. "She didn't give in easily. Didn't lie down and let death claim her. Didn't say it was her time to go. She cursed death and said if he wanted her, he would have to fight for her."

"That sounds like mother," Lyphnia said almost fondly. "What took her in the end?"

"Age, I believe. It's a miracle she lasted this long, especially without slowing and getting stone scales like most elders." He picked at the hem of his robe's sleeve. "She was sick, and the healers couldn't find anything wrong with her, or make her better. I think she knew she was dying, and accepted it, but wasn't happy about it. The healers said she lasted longer than she should have. She called for me, and I think she refused to go until one of her children was with her."

Lyphnia nodded solemnly and spoke softly. "We were her reason for living. We were her purpose. It doesn't surprise me that she wanted one of us there to carry her ashes." She tilted her head then to look at him. He saw the movement out of the corner of his eye, but kept his gaze fixed on the horizon. "Why did she choose you?" she asked, not angry or upset or bitter. Merely curious.

"I think I was the closest at the time, and she knew she wouldn't last long enough for one of us to make a longer journey."

"I think it was because you were her favorite."

Rajiah looked at her, startled. She regarded him calmly. Again, there was no bitterness in her voice. She was merely stating a fact. His lip curled. "I was not. She was on my tail for centuries, trying to mold me and prod me into following in her footsteps. She was disappointed in me when I went off on my own and stopped responding to her summons."

"You were still her favorite." Lyphnia said, eyes searching his. She lifted a hand, running her fingertips gently under his jaw, tilting his chin so she could examine his face. "The golden child. The young omega. The only omega she ever birthed. The rest of us were strong and powerful alphas, yes, and she was proud to have been our mother. But you were her favorite. You were the one she hoped would follow her example."

He swatted her hand away, face souring. "Yeah, and that turned out so well."

"She may have prodded you and pushed you, but she never forced you. She didn't chase you down and choose a mate for you, and we both know that she could have. But she let you go. She waited for you to make a choice. That's proof enough that you were her favorite."

Rajiah made a face and looked away. He knew his mother had had a soft spot for him, and that made her disappointment in him sting that much more. He was the golden child, destined for greatness. A greatness he never fulfilled because everything she wanted for him was nothing he wanted for himself.

"I think your father was also her favorite." Lyphnia continued. "She had many lovers and many mates, but most of them were chosen for their fertility and power. Your father was a dragon without a name and without a legacy, but she chose him nonetheless." She glanced at him again. "You look like him, you know."

"I know," he said softly. "Mother used to tell me." He'd never known his father. He had died in the wars and the Purge long before he could meet his only son. "I always thought you were her favorite," he said truthfully. "You're so much like her."

She laughed humorlessly. "Perhaps a little too much at times. We butted heads more often than not. But I would be foolish to say she wasn't proud of me. She was. She would be a fool not to. Other than her, I was the most powerful alpha female of our kind."

"You still are."

"I still am," she said, not bothering to hide her pride. "She was proud of my accomplishments, but I was never her favorite." Rajiah was silent, unsure of what to say to that admission. "Did she say anything in her last moments?"

Rajiah's lip curled, nose wrinkling. His stomach roiled unpleasantly at the memory. "She made me make her a promise."

"Oh?"

"I'll let you guess what that promise was."

"To find a mate," she said. It wasn't a question.

"To find a mate," he affirmed.

"Will you?"

He shrugged. "Only time will tell."

"This Summit is the best chance you have to assess what's left of our race."

"I know."

He knew, but he wasn't happy about it. He had promised his mother that he would try his best to find a mate and attempt to have children. He had promised, but he wasn't sure he could keep that promise. Finding an alpha willing to mate with him would be easy, of that much he was certain. But he didn't want just any mate. He wanted someone he actually felt a connection with. His mother had said that was a fool's idea. She had mated with plenty of dragons she hadn't loved.

But, deep in her eyes, he saw the sympathy. He saw the understanding. She knew how deep a mateship could be if there was a connection and love.

Rajiah tried to think about a perfect mate for him, tried to imagine the possibilities of what he might look like, tried to summon up an image of what he wanted. Yet all he could see were scales like the night and eyes like shadows in a snowstorm.

He flew back to the valley feeling both light and heavy.

Rajiah had spent a lot of his time during the last few centuries away from his own kind. Dragons were rarer than they had been, and in most cases, they were independent creatures. Dragons didn't live in packs like most shifters.

Their hierarchy consisted of the elders: wise, respected, and powerful, but without the youth, stamina, and strength to lead at the front lines of their race. Below them were dragon kings and queens, powerful dragons given the title by the Elders. And the Elders were very picky about who they bowed to. When dragons were more plentiful, there were more kings and queens. The world was split into factions, and each king and queen had their territory. They were the equivalent of pack leaders, of a pack's Alpha. The difference was the fact that dragons were stubborn and aggressive creatures by nature. Most couldn't stand to be around others for years at a time.

So dragons mostly lived on their own, either in their own territories or as roamers. They mostly lived as mated pairs or with close friends or family. Each dragon was bound to a king or queen, and those kings and queens were supposed to listen to the elders. So in a way, they formed a pack, but it was a pack that was widely spread, didn't live together, and gathered on occasions.

The Summit was one of those occasions.

There were many reasons for a Summit. In the past, they were usually for more light-hearted occasions. Summits were held in celebration of their kind, as a way to gather and see those they hadn't seen in years. To feast and dance and have tournaments and simply revel in being a dragon. Mates were found, mateships were celebrated, newly presented youths were shown off, and children were introduced.

Nowadays, Summits were called for much more melancholy reasons: for important decisions to be made. This Summit, for example, was the most important one in a millennium or two. All the Elders, or at least the important ones who weren't hidden away in caves, were dead. There was only one remaining official dragon king and queen pair. Dragon kind had decisions to make about their future.

Yet, despite the apprehensive atmosphere, a Summit was still a Summit. And a Summit was nothing if not a party.

A two-week long party to be precise, beginning on the third full moon since the call went out. There would be meetings, of course, to determine their future, but between those meetings there would be feasts and music and dances and tournaments.

In the weeks that followed Rajiah's arrival, dragons poured into the valley from all over the globe. Dragons of all shapes and sizes and colors. Males and females. Alphas, betas, and omegas. The old and the young. The battle worn and the summer children. They came in flocks, and they came alone. Some settled into the rooms at the castle and some chose to settle into the caves along the mountain sides that bordered the valley.

Dragons were everywhere, in human and beast form. Rajiah couldn't walk through the castle without running into one and couldn't look up at the sky without seeing the flash of light against scales.

It wasn't that he wasn't used to people. Rajiah may not have spent a lot of time around his own kind, but he also hadn't been alone. He had spent a lot of his time among other shifters, roaming around the world, spending months and years with different packs. He'd been with wolves and tigers, eagles and serpents, foxes and lions. Anything and everything in between. He wasn't shy around them. He loved people.

Yet, he found himself seeking sanctuary more often than not when confronted with his own kind. The weeks passed sluggishly, and he found refuge in the valley more and more often, speaking with and spending time with the local shifters who had moved there for sanctuary. He didn't see much of Lyphnia or Arulean in that time. It wasn't surprising. They were both busy.

Still, he often found his eyes upturned when dragons passed, or glancing at movement in the halls, searching before he even realized who he was searching for, who he was trying to catch a glimpse of. Each time, disappointment filled his gut, churning before he forced it down and away.

It was an unconscious reaction, and one that he wasn't happy to have. He wasn't a fool. He knew exactly what that feeling meant. He knew exactly what was growing inside him. And he knew exactly where this was going if he didn't put a stop to it immediately. Just as he knew it wasn't his place to have this feeling at all.

There were some things and some people who were simply off limits, and Arulean was at the top of that list.

Rajiah had forgotten just how boisterous and loud his own kind could be. The Summit wasn't set to begin for a few more days, but the castle was full of dragons. He hadn't seen so many in one place in centuries. And while some of them preferred to go out and hunt on their own, most chose to eat in the castles dining hall at the nightly feast.

Tables filled the room, each packed with people. The variety in the room was astounding. Their human forms were just as varied and beautiful as their dragon forms. The tables were packed with food and dishes and plates. Servants roamed the room, making sure the wine and ale kept coming.

Energy filled the room, buzzing and near sparking as it crackled along his skin. Auras clashed. So many presences that it was hard to tell one from the other, but each one as strong and stubborn on its own. The only thing that drowned them all out was the twin Auras of black and red coming from the head table at the far end of the room. Rajiah wasn't even sure how the lesser shifters could stand to be in the room full of dragons without being forced to their knees by the sheer weight of the energy.

As Rajiah was finding out, there were benefits and drawbacks to being related to both Lyphnia Scarlet and the Great Mother. He was given a seat at the head table, raised above the rest on a dais at the back of the hall during group meals. Seated next to Lyphnia, he was separated from the main herd of dragons at the tables below. This was a benefit. It looked like chaos down there, and as an unmated omega with a well-known lineage and somewhat of a mystery to dragon kin due to his lack of previous interaction with them, he was a novelty that wouldn't go unnoticed. Being separated from the crowd meant he didn't have to worry about people approaching him while he ate or swarming him in an attempt to vie for his attention.

The drawback, however, was that he was now easily on display. It was hard to dissolve into the background like he usually did when he was set up on a near literal pedestal next to the dragon queen herself. They might not look alike, but he was willing to bet every dragon in the room knew exactly who and what he was.

He did his best to shrink in his seat, to let the more boisterous personalities around him take center stage. Still, he felt eyes on him. He caught the glances of curious men and envious women. He ignored them all, but he knew that as soon as the safety of the table was removed and he was out from under Lyphnia's intimidating presence, he would be swarmed just as he feared.

He wasn't sure if Lyphnia was the source of it, or if everyone had just assumed, but word of his free status had spread like wildfire. He heard it in whispers, he saw it in the way people stared, in the way they stopped talking as he passed, felt it in the lustful and greedy stares of Alphas.

He was regretting ever giving into his mother's summons.

He spent his time eating as quickly as possible, ignoring the looks sent his way, caught between making awkward, idle conversation with Lyphnia (who was alternating between sending snide remarks toward Arulean and ignoring him altogether) and an entirely uncomfortable conversation with the Alpha placed on his other side (a man who was apparently a battle-worn general during the Purge, of a well-known lineage, father of many, and currently without a mate, as he was eager to slip into conversation time and time again).

Once the feast started to die down, people started mingling more. They drifted out to the courtyard and to the emptier halls set up with dessert and drink tables along the side, allowing for an open floor plan for congregating and socializing. Rajiah waited until Lyphnia excused herself from the table before slipping away himself.

The general beside him, whose name he never bothered to learn, was vying for his attention, but he excused himself with a small smile, saying he had to relieve himself before rejoining the festivities. The man smiled at that, winking and saying he'd be waiting. Rajiah's smile fell as soon as he turned around. He hurried out the back entrance behind the high table to avoid passing by any other dragons who wanted his attention. The back hall was mostly empty, with just servants hurrying to and fro. Rajiah smiled at a few of them, but mostly kept his head down and his eyes averted.

As soon as no one was around, he slipped up the lesser-used staircase toward the back of the castle. It didn't take long for the noise to be left behind. The castle was big, and built sturdily. Sounds echoed along its cavernous halls. Rajiah put enough space between him and the great hall that the sounds became little more than white noise in the distance.

He was sure some would notice his absence, but he didn't quite care. He didn't think anyone would come looking for him, and if they did, they wouldn't be able to find him. If anything, they would assume he was lost somewhere in the crowd and continue to search for him there. But with so many dragons in one area, it was near impossible to pinpoint anyone by scent or aura, save for Arulean and Lyphnia. His sister might be bothered by his absence, and he'd probably receive a stern talk on the morrow about socializing with his own people in order to choose a mate, but she had other dragons to talk to and he knew she wouldn't leave to find him.

He wandered the corridors on the upper levels. With the dragons at the feast and most of the servants helping down there as well, the rest of the castle was abandoned. It should have given him an eerie feeling, but he was oddly comfortable, liking the thrill of adventure and exploring a place that could never fully be explored. When he was younger and newly presented, he'd spent most of his time wandering the halls and avoiding socializing as his family insisted. He learned how to hide in all the nooks and crannies then. The castle had plenty.

It was a place full of surprises, and that was what kept the mystery and wonder alive.

He ran his hands along the walls, ghosting them over tables and door frames. He had no destination in mind, and he wasn't surprised when his feet led him to the library. It had often been his favorite place to hide when he was last here. So few people frequented the library, but it held a treasure trove of knowledge just begging to be read.

He pushed a door open, slipping inside before letting it close behind him. He then took a moment to lean back against the large oak doors and simply gape. While the size of the room hadn't changed, the contents of the room had damn near tripled. The collection hadn't been small to begin with, but now the floor-to-ceiling shelves were stuffed to the brim, cubbies with scrolls over flowing, tables with stacked books and scrolls littering the tops. He walked through the room slowly, weaving through bookshelves and reverently letting his fingers caress the bindings. Binding was still a relatively new phenomenon, and expensive, too, but Arulean had spared no expense in stocking his library.

Rajiah stepped up to a stand on which a heavy volume lay open, and idly flipped through the pages. It was in the language of the ancients, a language of old dragon tongue that was slowly fading through the centuries. From what he could tell by skimming, the book was a history of their kind, documented and no doubt copied from century-old scrolls.

The library was built with thick walls to block out most of the sound from the castle, with thick doors to muffle the noise from the hallway. Which is how he found himself with little warning as voices suddenly became apparent.

Voices, footsteps, slowly getting louder. His head snapped up, and he immediately reached out with his mind and senses to ascertain who it was. He noticed Arulean's presence immediately. It was hard not to. The man was one of the two auras that functioned as practical beacons around the castle. He was speaking with someone in hushed tones, the subject of their conversation lost through the wall. But they were definitely getting louder.

Without giving it much thought, he ducked further into the library, hiding himself among the shelves and beneath one of the desks to obscure him from view. Out of habit, he touched his wrists and his neck, making sure he still wore his scent-dimming jewelry. He also dimmed his own aura, making it as meek and unnoticeable as possible. The years spent traveling on his own had taught him how to make himself disappear. He couldn't make everything go away completely, but he knew how to make his own presence so subtle that it often went overlooked.

He startled and stilled when the doors to the library opened and suddenly the voices were thrown into audible clarity.

"—just don't like it, Arulean," said a gruff voice, deep and hoarse with a pleasant cadence and the ease of familiarity. He had a hard time placing it. The man's scent and presence was overshadowed by Arulean, and Rajiah didn't know enough of his kind to place it by voice alone.

"You do not have to like it," came Arulean's voice, dark and smooth, with a cadence of its own like a steady river. Powerful but deceptively calm. Danger lurked below those waters, but the surface looked peaceful as a pool. "The fact remains that this is our reality. My reality."

"She is not who she used to be." The man persisted. The doors closed behind them and the voices came deeper into the library. Rajiah pushed himself into the nook beneath the desk, keeping his breathing steady and shallow as his fingers nervously played with his scent blocking bands.

"I am no longer who I used to be."

"Exactly! No one would blame you if you found another. Most are surprised you don't have several mates already. You're the most powerful male alpha of our kind right now. We need you—"

"You need me to keep her on a tight leash. Not to spread my seed."

"You have proven to be fertile in the past."

"And not anymore." His voice grew sharper with irritation. It was a small flare of anger that Rajiah wasn't used to hearing from him. Especially not recently, when everything about the man was carefully calm and cold.

"Arulean, I'm sorry, but you can't dwell on the past."

"The past is what shapes us. The past is what I hope to never repeat. I keep it close so we can learn from it."

"But living in the past gives you a fractured existence. I see you now, Arulean, and you look like you're not entirely here. Half your mind is always away. I see the shadows in your eyes, the ghosts on your face. You need to let them lie and live for the future."

"I am living for the future!" the Alpha snapped. "The future is what haunts me! It is on my mind near constantly. I know what I have to do, and you cannot persuade me to do otherwise. I have given this far too much thought. I know what my path holds."

"Your path will lead to your unhappiness."

"My happiness is not important."

"It is."

"Not when the fate of our entire race is on my shoulders." He sighed. "I once lived for happiness, for myself, and that got us to where we are today. I cannot afford to live like that anymore. I am not that young naive dragon any longer."

"You can allow yourself some semblance of happiness."

"Perhaps... but not in the way you suggest."

"She cares nothing for you, Arulean. Anyone with eyes can see it."

"That does not matter."

"To hell with that! She looks upon you with disdain. That is not the look of a mate, Arulean. It is the look of a cobra poised to strike."

"She will not harm me, nor will she leave me."

"You don't know--"

"Gerrald." Arulean snapped, effectively silencing the man. Gerrald. Recognition sparked. Gerrald Onyx, Arulean's younger brother, second-in-command during the wars, and one of the only ones close enough to him to speak so openly. "I know so. I am half of her power, and she craves power above all else. It is what drew her to me to begin with. Without me, she loses half of her influence. She will not harm or leave me."

"Just usurp your ideas and authority," Gerrald sneered.

"I can handle her. She is not quite so crafty as she likes to think she is."

"She's dangerous."

"She is. She is passionate about her opinions, and that makes her very dangerous indeed. But it is nothing I cannot handle or curb."

Gerrald sighed, a sound of resignation that seemed to echo about the room, then fading to silence. They were close. Too close for comfort. "I just don't like seeing you this way," he said softly, almost reproachfully.

"And which way would that be?"

"You know which way. You walk these halls like a ghost, Arulean, when you used to rule your domain with a fire of life that not even the sun could match. She brings you no happiness. If anything, she worsens your condition."

There was movement, the sound of someone leaning back against the desk, a defeated but resigned sigh. Rajiah stiffened, skin prickling and itching, but he dared not to move. "We have been over this. How I feel does not matter. Not anymore. Besides, I am not quite sure happiness is something I deserve anymore."

"Nothing was your fault. You couldn't do anything to stop it, and you know that."

"Perhaps," He said softly. "But I cannot help but feel I could have done more to keep it from getting so bad."

"You don't need to keep suffering for past mistakes. Allow yourself to be happy." Gerrald continued quickly, cutting off another protest. "I'm not saying drop everything. I'm saying if happiness comes your way, be open to it."

Another sigh. "We will see."

"Promise me you won't run from happiness."

"Gerrald--"

"Promise me, Arulean."

"I will not break our mateship."

A sigh from Gerrald this time. "I'm not saying—just ... don't let her hold you back."

"Fine."

"Thank you."

There was a pause, a silence, a drumming of fingers on the thick wood of the desk above him. There was a shift in Arulean's aura, a shift in his scent. It was subtle, but noticeable. "Perhaps you should return to the festivities." There was a shift in his voice. Something far too calm to be natural, not when just previously they had been speaking with a frank openness and familiarity. Rajiah stiffened, breath stilling.

Gerrald paused, apparently noticing the shift judging from the mild confusion in his voice when he spoke. "Will you be joining me?"

"I have something that needs attending to. I will return later."

"If you don't, Lyphnia will use that against you..."

"I do not need to be there for everyone to know my presence."

"She will use this as time to plant seeds of doubt."

"I will be there later."

"Arulean--"

"I promise I am not locking myself away again. Now if you will excuse me..." His voice was stern, stiff, and allowed no argument. Gerrald huffed, and Rajiah could only imagine the disgruntled look on the gruff man's scarred face. But then there were retreating footsteps, the door opening and closing, and the silence. Fingers continued to drum atop the desk in a steady pattern. Rajiah held his breath. He waited, prayed, for Arulean to move and go about his business, but he never did.

"I know you're there." His voice was chillingly calm, low, and sent shivers straight down his spine. The fingers continued to tap. Rajiah didn't move. He wasn't sure he could. He certainly couldn't breathe. "You might as well show yourself."

Tension stretched, taut as a bowstring ready to snap. Had Arulean been anyone else, he might have tried to call his bluff, continue to hide, hope he wasn't found. But if anyone could sense him past his precautions, it was this man.

Steeling himself, he took a deep breath, feeling the adrenaline rush through his system, giving him courage. Settling himself into a passive, casual, calm, he pushed himself out from under the desk and stood.

Arulean was leaning back against the edge of the desk, hands back on the wood and fingers tapping, legs stretched out in front of him and crossed at the ankles. His back was to Rajiah, and he didn't turn around. That, in and of itself, was a blatant show of power, proving that he didn't feel Rajiah was enough of a threat, so it was acceptable to put his back to him. He was right, but it still made his hackles rise at the disrespect.

They were both silent for a long moment, tension thick and apprehension clawing its way down his throat. He crossed his arms over his chest, leaning his weight to one hip and adopting a position of defensive nonchalance. He stopped holding back his aura, letting it simmer and shine as it wanted. He hadn't done anything wrong, and he wasn't going to act like he had.

"What are you doing in my library?" The voice was the same deceptive calm, deep but icy at its core. It was a voice used to intimidate, but it only made Rajiah's annoyance rise. He refused to submit to anyone. Not Lyphnia, not his own mother, and certainly not Arulean.

"I wasn't aware it was yours." He said calmly, voice just as hard.

Arulean turned his head at that, glancing at Rajiah over his shoulder. He hated to admit the hitch in his breath when he met those dark eyes. Arulean looked him over, one eyebrow raised. "It is my castle," he said, perfectly neutral.

"And so visitors aren't allowed in the library?" Rajiah asked, raising an eyebrow to mirror him. "Typically, libraries are public spaces."

"No one visits the library except for me," Arulean said matter of factly.

"Does that mean no one is allowed?"

A pause. "No," He turned around more fully, eyeing Rajiah with more curiosity, but still with closed-off assessment. "But no one visits the library."

"I do."

"You never have before."

"I used to come in here whenever I visited." He admitted, shifting his weight under Arulean's heavy gaze and letting his eyes roam the bookshelves. "It's quiet in here ... peaceful. It's a good place to escape when the others are overwhelming."

It was quiet for a moment, and then Arulean nodded. "It is. That is often why I come here. I also enjoy reading. The knowledge this room contains is vast, but so few are eager to learn." He said, gesturing widely at the room.

"I like reading, too." Arulean looked at him like he didn't quite believe him.

Rajiah scowled. "I do!"

Arulean looked him over, brows furrowing just slightly. "You are a peculiar one, Rajiah Bronze."

He didn't know what to say to that, so instead he asked, "How did you know I was there?"

Arulean pushed off the desk, loosely clasping his hands behind his back as he strode over to the book stand Rajiah had been standing near, idly flipping back through the pages. "I was reading this earlier, and I noticed it was no longer on the page I had left it on." He didn't look up as his hands traced words on the page. Rajiah found himself transfixed by those long, slender fingers. The thought came unbidden, of what those fingers would feel like against his skin, caressing him with the same amount of tenderness and care. "I could smell traces of someone, but I had assumed he had been in here earlier. It wasn't until I was seated there that I noticed your presence. It was subtle at first, nearly drowned out by Gerrald and I." He looked at Rajiah then, dark eyes sharp and suspicious. "It is... very peculiar for a dragon."

Rajiah shrugged. "I'm very good at hiding myself."

"I noticed." He turned back to the book, flipping a page. But while he looked nonchalant, Rajiah could still feel the tension in the room. "But tell me, why do you have need to hide in the first place." Rajiah opened his mouth to respond, but snapped it shut when he didn't know what to say. Arulean continued. "As you have stated, the library is a public, if seldom used, place. So why should you hide beneath a desk when my brother and I come?" He looked at Rajiah then, eyes sharp and lips pursed into the smallest of frowns. The hostility was sudden enough to make him freeze. "Unless you are here for ill-begotten purposes."

Rajiah gaped, eyes wide and brows furrowed. "Like what?" He asked, incredulous.

Arulean closed the book gently but firmly, letting the sound echo dully in the room. "Like spying for your sister."

"What?"

He turned toward him. "Like listening in on private conversations to gather information."

"I'm not—"

He took a step forward. "Like positioning yourself in a space that only I frequent and looking through my most recent research for clues."

"I wasn't--"

Several more steps, closing the distance between them in long, fluid strides. "Like reporting back to your sister regarding my movements."

"Will you stop--"

Arulean stopped right in front of him. They were toe-to-toe, and Rajiah had to crane his neck back to look up at the taller man, but he refused to back down. Not when these accusations were being thrown at him. Not when Arulean was accusatory and angry and was making Rajiah's defenses act up. He stood his ground, his own anger increasing.

Then Arulean bent down, and suddenly their faces were very close. Too close. The scent of him, strong and powerful, smoke and musk, like cool nights and campfires, washed over him. Rajiah knew the scent of alphas. He could admit to being lured in by it. He could admit that alphas smelled good. It was his biology to be attracted to it. But never had an alpha's scent hit him with enough force to leave his mouth dry, his knees weak, and cause heat to go spiraling through his gut. He could do little more than gape, trying to get a handle on himself.

"Like working with your sister to undermine my authority." Arulean's breath ghosted over Rajiah's face, caressing his cheeks, his lips. His stomach tied itself in knots, and he found it hard to breathe.

Only through the pure force of indignant anger was Rajiah able to keep himself from grabbing Arulean by the face and dragging him forward.

"I'm not working for my sister," he spat, putting a hard emphasis on each word as he scowled. His hands clenched into tight fists, the pain of his nails digging into his palms keeping him grounded.

Arulean was still far too close, his dark eyes searching Rajiah's. The dim lighting made it difficult to see the line between iris and pupil, even at this distance. The bridge of his brows pinched just a fraction. "She is ... your sister?" It was said like a question, flavored with confusion.

Rajiah scoffed. "Yes, and?"

Arulean leaned back, face blank as he looked over Rajiah's face. "You are not loyal to her?" he asked slowly, as if the question tasted odd on his tongue.

Rajiah rolled his eyes. "She's my sister, but she's not my master."

Both Arulean's eyebrows went up at that. "Blood does not bind you?"

Rajiah's lips quirked up at that, his scowl fading into something more akin to amusement. "You don't know much about me, do you?" he asked dryly.

"I admit, I do not. It is not often Lyphnia speaks of you or her family," he paused, and then added. "Or much to me at all."

Rajiah's smile curved wider as he tilted his head to the side, wavy locks falling across his forehead as he stared up at the other dragon. "Not even my mother could control me."

"That ... must have bothered her greatly."

The Great Mother had been known for being a very controlling alpha. Most of her children, and most of those she met, were quickly put under her thumb. She had butted heads with Lyphnia more times than he could count, but that was because they were far too similar. In the end, she couldn't help but be proud of what her daughter had accomplished and how powerful she had become. Rajiah had been another person she couldn't control, but one she hadn't tried too hard with. He had always thought it was because she considered him a lost cause. But now, with Lyphnia's words echoing in his memory, he was starting to wonder if it was indeed because he was a favorite.

"It did."

Arulean stepped back, regarding Rajiah with an expression that the latter couldn't read. "Who are you loyal to then, Rajiah Bronze?"

Rajiah didn't hesitate. "Myself." He lifted his chin. "And our kind."

"To dragons." He tilted his head just a fraction, giving Rajiah a very pointed look. "To the Elders or the kings and queens?"

"Neither," Rajiah said, lip curling. "I don't mean dragons. I mean all shifters."

Arulean remained silent at that, but he blinked a couple times to show his bafflement.

Rajiah continued, "They suffer just as much, if not more so, than we do. We're all shifters, and I want what's best for all of us." His lip curled into a sneer. "None of this 'we're better than them' talk."

"You ... do realize Lyphnia's stance on the subject of lesser shifters?" Arulean asked cautiously.

Rajiah rolled his eyes. "I'm aware. It's not like she hides her opinions."

"So you do not agree with her on most points?"

He threw his hands up in the air with an exasperated sound. "That's what I've been trying to tell you!"

"Then what were you doing in my library?"

"I told you! I came here to get away from everyone!"

"Then why did you hide?"

Rajiah crossed his arms over his chest, shrugging one shoulder. He looked away, down to the side as he mumbled. "I don't know. Habit, I guess. I don't like being noticed."

"You are very noticeable." He said so bluntly, and with an odd edge to it that made heat rise to Rajiah's cheeks. He scowled, trying to force down the flush.

Before he could speak again, however, they both heard the sudden and sharp tap of footsteps in the hall. They both whipped their heads around to look at the door. Heels on stone, sharp quick pace. There were only a few things that could mean. Sure enough, when Rajiah reached out hesitantly, he felt the fiery crimson aura of his sister.

His eyes widened. "Oh no," He whispered, whipping around to Arulean, one hand already resting on the desk. "Don't tell her I'm here, please."

He eyed him curiously. "Why?"

"She'll drag me back downstairs and force me to talk to suitors. I've had enough hungry eyes on me tonight, and if I'm forced to listen to one more story of self-imposed bravery from an egotistical alpha's mouth, I might just snap." He met Arulean's eyes, pleading silently, and then whispered, "Please."

Arulean regarded him for a moment, and then nodded quickly. "Fine. Get under the desk again. I'll cover your tracks."

"What if she notices me like you did?"

Arulean scoffed. "She is far too enamored with herself to notice much of anything else."

Rajiah snorted. He had no reason to argue that particular point. He ducked beneath the desk, assuming his previous position just as the doors to the library opened with far more force than necessary.

"Arulean," came Lyphnia's greeting, though it sounded almost like an accusation. It was loud in the otherwise quiet space.

Arulean shifted so he was standing on the opposite side of the desk from the door, his legs blocking the opening to Raji-ah's hidden nook. He could hear the man idly sorting through a few books on the desk. "Lyphnia," he said sounding bored.

"Where are you? This place is needlessly huge."

"Over here," he said, raising his volume just a fraction. "And it is not too large. If anything, it is too small for my growing collection."

Her heels were sharp against the floor as she strode across the room. "What does a dragon need with dusty old books? We are creatures of action and fire, not idleness and paper."

"We are wise creatures, and, to be such, we must learn. The past has plenty to teach us."

He could practically hear his sister rolling her eyes. "Never mind that, I didn't come here to argue with you again about your hoard," she said, sneering. She paused, then asked a little too evenly. "Why are you here and not at the festivities with our people?"

"Gerrald wanted a word with me in private."

"Gerrald? He's not here."

"He just left."

"What did he wish to speak with you about?"

"Private matters, Lyphnia."

She hummed irritated, and Rajiah nearly jumped when he heard her put her hands on the top of the desk, opposite Arulean. When she spoke again, her voice was pitched low. "There was once a time when there were no matters private enough to be secrets between us," she purred. Rajiah felt his hair stand on end.

"Those times are long gone, Lyphnia." Arulean said, almost sadly, with a hint of irritation.

"Do they have to be, though? We can get them back... our spark shouldn't be that hard to rekindle, Arulean. You and I, we've always had it."

Something sickening and heavy solidified in Rajiah's gut. He struggled to keep his aura contained, but he doubted it mattered. Not with how brightly Lyphnia was shining at the moment. He glared at Arulean's legs, standing firm and solid. He imagined the man's stoic face.

For the sake of dragon-kind, he knew he should be hoping for them to become mates again in truth. He had heard rumors of the distance between them, but hadn't realized the full extent of it until he had witnessed it with his own eyes. They were mated still, but there was no warmth between them. He should want them back together. They were stronger united, and their kind needed strong leaders. Not to mention they had bred several children in their life-time, which was important with their species dying out as it was. He should have no reason to want them to remain so distant.

However, Rajiah felt nothing but relief when Arulean replied with chillingly brutal honesty, "I do not want it back, Lyphnia." His voice was soft, low, barely above a whisper, but it had the effect of a shout.

She slammed her hands on the desk, making Rajiah jump. "You are a fool, Arulean Black. A fool." She seethed.

He sighed. "Why are you here, Lyphnia? Surely, it is not to drag me back to the festivities. We both know you prefer to shine without me."

"I came to see if you had seen my brother," she said, still seething but her anger under better control.

Rajiah stiffened, breath stilling.

"Was he not at dinner?"

"He was, but then he slipped away and hasn't returned. Euwen Gold is looking for him."

"Euwen Gold?"

"Yes, the man has taken a liking to him. He hopes to woo him before any of the other Alphas. He said they had a delightful conversation during the feast, though I doubt it. Euwen isn't much of a conversationalist, and Rajiah is quick to bore."

"Already attempting to mate off your brother?"

"Not my idea," She said offhandedly. "It was my mother's dying wish that he find a mate. Which he'll never do if he keeps running away like this."

"I have not seen him."

"Would you tell me if you had?" she said with an edge of bitterness. "We are keeping secrets from one another now, after all."

"What reason do I have for keeping your brother from you?"

There was a long, tense silence where Rajiah could practically imagine them sizing each other up, looking for cracks in the other's mask. He barely dared to breathe, keeping every breath shallow and even. A finger traced one of the gold bands on his wrist.

Finally, Lyphnia broke the silence. "If you see him, please direct him back to the gathering."

"I will do so."

She spun around and strode out of the library, pace barely stopping to swing the door shut behind her with a muffled bang. They waited in silence, neither of them moving. Rajiah's heartbeat slowly returned to normal, his breaths coming easier.

"I believe it is safe to come out now." Arulean said, stepping away from the desk.

Rajiah crawled out and got to his feet, brushing off his clothes. "Thank you," He muttered, avoiding eye contact in favor of straightening out his garments.

"Are you certain you do not wish to return to Euwen Gold?"

Rajiah's head snapped up, eyes locking onto that dark gaze. He gaped, nose crinkling in disgust. "Why in hell would I want to..." His words trailed off. While Arulean's voice had been the same as it always was, there was something glinting in his eyes, a tugging at the corner of his lips. Reality hit Rajiah hard, knocking the breath from his lungs with a surprised laugh. He felt his lips curling into a small smile. "By the Elders, did you just tease me? Is the great Arulean Black making jokes?"

He chuckled, shoulders shaking slightly. The sound was deep and rumbling and sent shivers down his spine as warmth pooled in his gut. He liked that sound a lot. Perhaps too much. "I have been known to do that from time to time."

"It's a damn miracle is what it is."

"I suppose you won't be attending the rest of the festivities then?"

"I had no plans to, no."

"Perhaps you would like some help finding books that might interest you?" Arulean said, gesturing widely at the shelves. "I know this library through and through. I could be of assistance."

Rajiah found his smile widening as he said softly, a little breathlessly, "Yeah, I'd like that."

Neither of them made it back to the gathering that evening.

CHAPTER
FIVE

The official start of The Summit was a momentous occasion. The castle practically hummed with energy the entire day leading up to the full moon. The valley was alight with buzzing from hundreds of dragons and other shifters eagerly awaiting the night. Everyone seemed to run automatically, going through the motions of the day without fully being there mentally. Even the conversations that happened were said and heard with half an ear. It was as if the entire population of the valley was in a daze that hazed over their reality as they waited.

As the sun set, the dragons began to gather in the large flight field outside the castle. Hundreds, if not thousands, of people, standing around in various stages of undress, waiting and watching, heads tilted toward the sky.

Arulean and Lyphnia stood in the center of the field as darkness faded over the valley. They were both naked, standing tall and proud with chins tilted upward. There was more distance between them than was typical of mates, but no one said anything. Their auras burned brightly, subduing the crowd and drawing them in all at once.

Rajiah stood close, but melded into the crowd. Lyphnia wanted him close at her side as a show of the power and authority of their lineage, but once she had stepped out of her clothes and up to Arulean, the feeling of the approaching full moon vibrating through her system, she hadn't noticed when Rajiah had stepped back to blend among the people.

His eyes were on Arulean as his fingers idly traced the

outline of the thick gold choker that hung around his neck. Arulean stood tall and proud, body lean and muscles well-defined. Pale skin marred with long healed scars and the dips and valleys of his muscles beneath his flesh. His shoulders and chest were broad, hips slim, with powerful thighs. His dark hair was swept back from his forehead, wind caressing the locks to give them a gentle sway.

He was beautiful, and it was a fact that Rajiah was quickly becoming very aware of. He was indisputably attracted to the man, but he didn't think that was entirely his fault. Plenty of men and women must be attracted to him. He was handsome and powerful and a perfect specimen of a dragon. He was, biologically, the perfect mate, and he set Rajiah's insides aflame.

The problem was that Rajiah couldn't have him. Not only was he mated to Rajiah's sister, but he had stated to his brother that he had no plans on taking another mate. Lyphnia would be his one and only, despite the dissonance between them.

That, however, didn't stop Rajiah from wanting him. It was a strange sensation. He had been attracted physically to alphas before, but it had never been difficult to resist them. It had never been hard to say no. He found himself drawn to Arulean like a moth to a flame, so willing to fly straight into his own demise.

He could smell Arulean's scent on the wind, dark and tantalizing, burning his senses and making his hair stand on end. His mouth practically watered and his inner dragon shifted, rearing its head with the nearness of the full moon and the desire for a potential mate. Not just any mate.

His dragon wanted Arulean Black.

He gritted his teeth, clenching his jaw and digging his nails into his palm.

With the sun gone, the moon was rising. He felt it. The heaviness of his bones, the crack in his joints, the shifting of his muscles beneath his too tight skin, the press of his wings, skeletal like bones pressing against the paper thinness of the skin on his back. It ached, it hurt, but he knew the release would be so, so good.

At once, the crowd in the field seemed to shift, everyone anxiously restless as they stripped off the rest of their clothes. Rajiah joined them, slipping easily out of his pants and tunic, his boots having already been abandoned in the castle. Last to come off was his jewelry, he wore heavy gold bands and chains on his wrists and around his neck. Some of them were for show, but there were some that were scent blockers. They contained heavy elements, herbs, and magic charms to block out most of the pheromones from the scent glands at his wrists and neck. It helped him stay hidden, helped him move among lesser shifters and his own kind without drawing attention to himself.

For he was a child of the Great Mother, the only male omega she ever birthed, and with her strength came a great gift and a great curse: his scent was strong. It was strong and powerful to indicate his lineage and his supposed fertility as an omega. As an unattached omega, his scent was deliciously alluring, and it hadn't taken long for him to find measures to counterbalance that.

He folded the jewelry carefully in his clothes and set them aside. Standing up straight, the wind shifted. He felt it caress his back, his sides, ruffling his hair, carrying his scent toward the center of the field.

He saw several dragons turn in his direction, several alphas standing up straight, eyes finding him, nostrils flaring. His attention, however, was on Arulean. He saw the moment his scent reached him, saw something in his expression darken, saw his eyes tear themselves away from the sky, saw that gaze settle on him. Suddenly, the whole field disappeared. Breath caught in his throat at the gleam of hunger in the Alpha's eyes, the odd stiffness with which he stood, the tension in the air.

The moment stretched, brief and fleeting, yet immensely powerful and leaving Rajiah both weak at the knees and standing straight with confidence.

Then the moon came out and Arulean's attention returned to the occasion.

He and Lyphnia turned toward each other, eyes aglow and smoke drifting from their skin into the night air. Everyone on the field seemed to hold their breath as the king and queen crouched. Energy swirled around them, burning in the air. When they leapt, the ground splintered and cracked beneath them with the force, creating two small craters where their bodies had been as they rocketed upward. They shifted in the air, smoke swirling as their flesh burned away to make room for scales, their bodies lengthening and growing, wings bursting forth from their backs. They spread them wide, pumping the air as they shot straight upward.

He watched, breathless, as the two dragons swirled around each other, circling the field, black and red, shadow and blood against the night sky. Then they both opened their massive jaws and let loose a mighty roar in tandem that shook through the valley, vibrating mountainsides and shuddering through every shifter, down to their bones.

The two dragons swirled together before shooting off and away, moving toward the mountains.

The spell that kept the dragons on the ground and breathless broke. One by one and then all in rapid succession, dragons shot into the air in a similar fashion, shifting in the air as they took to the sky. Roars filled the air, creating rockslides and avalanches in the distance, shaking the earth with their voices. It was deafening. It was liberating. It was magic.

Rajiah's wings burst from him in a rush of pleasure. He spun upward, spiraling into the sky, pumping his wings harder, gaining speed. He joined the herd of dragons flying after Arulean and Lyphnia as they led a lazy circle around the mountains that framed the valley.

They were a rainbow in the night, colors of their scales dark with shadows, but glistening in the moonlight, sparking against the darkness. So many of them, all shapes and sizes, males and females, alphas, betas, and omegas, old and young. They flew together, a stream of dragons in a thick mass follow their king and queen.

After everyone was in the air, they circled the valley several more times before Arulean and Lyphnia suddenly climbed higher and dove out over the mountain range. There was a chorus of deep, rumbling voices as the flock of dragons followed.

The flight was chaos.

Dragons swirled and dove around each other, chasing and leading, gliding and climbing and diving. They swarmed out over the mountains, far enough from human civilization to be safe. They played in the air, danced in the clouds, flew low enough to let their claws brush the treetops, bounced off cliffs and mountains. They darted through the air, a cacophony of sounds accompanying them.

Above them flew Arulean and Lyphnia. The two darted and swirled around each other, neither one overtaking the other and neither one getting too close. Once upon a time, when Rajiah had visited the castle in his youth, he had seen them fly together on a full moon. They had been beautiful, two scaled creatures entertained and moving as one. They were constantly close, moving as if predicting the other's movements, flying high, embracing, and falling to the earth together. It had been a beautiful display of mateship.

It was more apparent in that moment than on any other that they were two rulers who ruled side by side, but did not love. Not anymore. He could see the hints of it, the echoes of a time when they had. He could see it in the way they still seemed to know each other's movements, in the way they had known patterns and kept pace with each other, but those were only echoes in the vast distance between them.

Rajiah had been watching them from a respectable distance, but a flash of dark, golden scales cut off his path, forcing him to pull up short. He hovered in the air, glaring at the large body of the alpha known as Euwen Gold. He was an impressive alpha, Rajiah would give him that. Euwen was strong in body and scent, and part of him stirred. But it was nothing compared to the desire he felt for the dragon king.

His lips curled away from his teeth in a warning snarl, but the larger dragon only sneered back, coiling his body closer. Rajiah snapped at the air before twisting away, curling down and around him before rising high and fast. Euwen followed, much to Rajiah's annoyance. He danced through the sky, trying to lose the larger Alpha in the crowd, but when he twisted his head around to look, he found that instead of losing an Alpha, he had gained several more pursuers.

Something in him came alive at the sight of that. Several alphas, each strong and powerful, chasing his scent, following on his tail. He reveled in that, a strange sense of power that he'd never truly felt before. The power that came with being a desired omega, young, fertile and unmated. The power that came with being wanted. Something confident overcame him, some part of him that wanted to be wanted, and liked it.

If those alphas wanted a chase, he would give them a chase.

He tilted his wings, lifting up high and spinning to face them, treading air. They pulled up short, shoving each other and watching him curiously. If Rajiah could grin, he would have. Something sly and seductive and cocky. As it stood, he was sure the pheromones he was producing in his rush of excitement were getting the message across just fine, if the responding scents from the alphas was anything to go by.

With a playful flick of his tail and a graceful roll of his body, he clamped his wings close to his body and went into a sudden nosedive. The alphas scrambled to follow.

Wind rushed past his ears, howling off his scales. He dove straight for a lake, flaring out his wings only at the last moment, rippling the water and dragging his claws across the surface. He heard a splash behind him and snickered when he saw one of the alphas struggling out of the lake. They were hot on his trail, and so he sped up. Empowered by himself and by the full moon, he twisted and danced through the air, weaving through the congregation of dragons and leading his alphas on a merry chase.

There were a few females and omegas doing the same, but he

steered clear of them, unwilling to lose any of his own pursuers. He enjoyed the chase, but he had no intention of being caught. And with his natural speed, quick maneuvering, and unyielding energy, he was unlikely to be caught unwillingly. He dove low before rising high, spinning and weaving through others, diving straight for cliff faces and landing hard before pushing off to give a quick turn to his momentum. He chortled deep in his throat at his pursuers, occasionally glancing back to see their frustration at being unable to catch up, yet the eager desperation with which they continued, driven by hunger. He had gained several more through the course of his flight.

He was power.

He was desired.

He had all of these alphas wrapped around his claw.

And, he liked it.

He wore them out, let their desires run them ragged. Still he flew on, adrenaline and energy singing through his veins as the moonlight reflected off his scales.

He was a son of the Great Mother, and he was untouchable.

He lost track of time during his frantic flight, only focused on putting on a show. His body was sleek and flexible, pulling off aerial moves that he knew would impress. He lost himself in it, reveling in everything, in being a dragon.

Then the wind shifted and he caught a whiff of that scent again. The scent that was dark and smoky, chilling and molten. The scent that spoke of power and heat. The scent of an alpha, equally untouchable, but one he wanted very much to touch. The only one he would bend his convictions for.

The only one his dragon, drunk on sensation and pheromones, deemed worthy of him.

In a burst of brash confidence, Rajiah altered his course.

Arulean and Lyphnia flew high above the others, spinning and swirling in a wide circle above the mountains, far apart from one another as they looped above the clouds. Others joined them. Rajiah distantly recognized Gerrald Onyx near Arulean. There were a few others, big dragons, old and of impressive lineage. None of them got too close to either the king or queen.

None of them, except for Rajiah.

He rushed directly through the invisible circle they were outlining, pulling his trail of alphas after him, though they were far behind. He spun and twirled in an impressive display before curling down and around. He rushed past his sister, feeling her spark of irritation and reveling in it. He knew how much Lyphnia liked to be admired, how much she liked to be chased, and how frustrated she must be that it wouldn't happen as long as Arulean was around.

Under normal circumstances, he wouldn't have dared to anger her this way, but he wasn't quite in his right mind. He was drunk off the full moon, feeling powerful and brave.

In that fit of bravery, he spun toward Arulean, looping around him far closer than he should have dared, and playfully, tauntingly, teasingly batted him with his tail as he passed, spiraling away with a deep rumbling laugh in his throat. As he dove away, he twisted his neck back, eyes finding the large, black dragon. His flight had halted and he hovered in the air with steady beats of his massive wings. His eyes were dark as his scales, but they glistened as he watched Rajiah. But he didn't move and he didn't give chase.

And while he looked as irritated and unperturbed as a dragon could be, the wind brought him Arulean's scent, thick with desire and pheromones, clearly projecting his want despite holding himself back.

That was enough for Rajiah. A new, fresh wave of desire rippled through him, fueling his desire to keep away from his pursuing alphas. None of them would have him. None of them were worthy. None of them made his heart pound and heat coil in his belly. If he couldn't have Arulean, no one would have him.

He was untouchable, and he would remain that way.

The afternoon sun was far too bright for Rajiah's liking. He groaned against the burn against his eyelids, curling deeper into the blankets, burrowing into the dark haven of his bed . He was awake, though he didn't want to be. He could hear servants tiptoeing around the sitting room beyond his bed chamber, the clatter of dishes telling him that they were bringing him food and drink, setting him up water to wash with, and no doubt straightening the mess he had made when he had stumbled back through the doors last night, bumping into nearly everything in a blind and desperate, sleep-deprived daze to reach his bed.

He wasn't sure what the time was, but the sun was high. He hadn't reached his rooms until sunrise, when the moon was long gone from the sky and the first rays of light were peeking above the mountains into the valley.

He was exhausted, physically and mentally drained. He had led the chase nearly all night, pushing himself to the limit with what had seemed like an abundance of drunken energy to tire out the alphas who pursued him. It had worked. He flew them all ragged until they could fly no more and had to land before they crashed. And, after the last of them had dropped out of the sky, giving up their chase for the evening, Rajiah had flown onward, gliding on the wind and showing off that he was still there, still flying, still full of life where so many others had been forced to give way.

He had flown through the night, ignoring the ache in his wings and the burn of the muscles in his back. It was a pain he welcomed, an ache that meant he was alive, an ache of being a dragon. He had been one of the last to stumble back into the castle to his room at daybreak.

Last night he had felt invincible, powerful, untouchable by others or by exhaustion itself.

Now, he regretted everything.

His entire body ached. His joints were sore and felt swollen, his muscles tight and aching. Even his skin felt taut and tight and far too sensitive. There was not a part on him that wasn't suffering from the full-body ache of sheer exhaustion, but his back was the worst. The muscles around his shoulder blades burned fiercely whenever he moved, throbbing when he was still. He didn't fly much anymore. He did a lot of his traveling on the ground, spending his time with grounded shifters. He certainly didn't fly like he did last night.

He was drifting somewhere between consciousness and sleep, mind and senses hazy, when the doors to his rooms were thrown so wide they crashed against the stone walls. A familiar click of heels against the floor grated against his ears just as a familiar scent drifted under the cracks of the door to his bedchamber.

"You are dismissed," he heard Lyphnia say lazily, but with the odd sharpness of authority that she always had around lesser shifters and servants. There was a shuffle and then the doors closed softly. More pacing, a pause, and then her voice rang out, louder, "Rajiah, it's time to wake up."

He groaned softly, pulling the blankets tighter around him, hoping to dissolve into the dark nest he had created. Perhaps if he was quiet and still enough, she would leave.

"I know you're awake, dear brother. Come, you cannot spend the entire day in bed."

"The hell I can't..." He grumbled, but threw the blanket off anyway, ignoring the way his arms ached with the movement.

He threw his legs over the edge of the bed, raising his arms high over his head to stretch. The muscles in his back screamed in silent protest, his joints popping and bones aching. But the ache was oddly soothing. As much as it hurt, as exhausted as he was, it was the joyous ache of a good flight, of stretching his wings and pushing his body and being a dragon. It was a reminder of the freedom he had experienced.

He stood, slipping on loose pants that tightened around his calves and a loose tunic. He didn't bother with anything else as he padded to the door and pushed it open, running a hand through his hair to detangle some knots. The sitting room was much brighter than his own room, where the curtains were at least half pulled to block out some light.

He squinted against the glare, scowling as his eyes roamed the room. He found Lyphnia lounging in one of the large, plush chairs, legs crossed delicately and draped over one arm of the chair. She was idly picking at a bowl of grapes that had been left on the low table in front of her.

She grinned at him as he entered the room, eyes sharp as always as they took in his appearance, smile amused. "Good morning, sleeping prince."

He grunted, shuffling across the room to the privy. Once he had relieved himself and washed his face, running wet fingers through his hair to tame the wayward strands, he padded back out into the room feeling much more awake and much less like a disgruntled animal.

He practically threw himself into the lounge chair across the table from Lyphnia. While she draped herself elegantly and gracefully, he sprawled across the cushions and arms like a discarded towel.

"What brings you here so early?" he asked, reaching forward to pick up an apple and a knife.

"Do I need a reason to visit my baby brother?" she asked innocently, almost mockingly, as she plucked off a grape from the vine with delicate fingers before placing it into her mouth.

He eyed her with a raised eyebrow, expression unamused as he sliced off a piece of the apple. "No, but you usually have one. Especially this early after a full moon."

"It's not so early."

"It is for us, and you know it. I didn't get in until daybreak, and I'm willing to bet you didn't either."

She idly inspected her nails as she chewed, humming in acknowledgement. "Perhaps."

She might try to play coy, but he knew he was right. Had she and Arulean been active mates, they would have retired much, much earlier. As it stood, he was willing to bet she had stayed out nearly all night just to lord over her domain and to keep from going back to an empty bed.

"Nevertheless, I am here to check up on you, dear brother."

He raised an eyebrow, chewing slowly before answering. "Have I done something that would give you reason to check up on me?" he asked slowly, carefully, shifting through his memory of the previous night. He had been toeing the edge of being disrespectful towards her, but he doubted that was enough to warrant a visit. Especially one that seemed almost friendly.

"I witnessed your flight last night ..." She said offhandedly, slowly, picking at the grapes with nails that were filed to perfection. Rajiah felt himself stiffen, body going tense before he could force himself to relax. The knife stilled halfway through cutting off another slice. He stared at her, eyebrows raised and expectant. He couldn't tell from her tone whether she was upset or not. She let her words hang in silence for several more minutes before continuing. "I lost sight of you after a while. After all, it is not necessary for me to watch the entirety of your flight, as from what I could see, it was a long one."

He shrugged as nonchalantly as he could. "I wasn't going to let just anyone catch me." A small spark of stubborn pride welled up in his chest as he gazed at her steadily. "I won't settle for anyone not worthy of me."

She met his eye steadily, the small quirk in her lips almost proud as she nodded. "As is expected. You are a child of the Great Mother, after all. And my brother. A prince of great lineage. You shouldn't settle for just any riffraff. Still, there are several suitable mates among our ranks, most of whom are either unmated or looking for additional mates. There were ... a plethora in your entourage last night." There was a note of bitterness in her voice that she couldn't quite hide.

He continued to eat, eyes on the task at hand. "Were there?" He asked, trying not to bristle, He knew what her tone indicated, and he didn't like it. "I hadn't noticed."

She hummed idly. "Yes, you did seem a tad ... invested in the power held over them. As is your right, might I add." She added, tossing the grapes aside and pouring herself tea from the steaming pot on the table. "In my youth, I was much the same way. It's an exhilarating power to have over alphas. They are weak creatures when it comes down to brass tacks, and it is a phenomenal ability to wrap them around your finger like the pliable weaklings they are."

She pushed a cup toward him, and Rajiah took it with a small nod of thanks. They both sipped, silence settling over the room.

"It was ... fun." He said finally, after mulling over her statement.

She nodded, a small, knowing smirk curling over the rim of her cup. "It is," she said simply. "And quite addicting. I came here to see if you had allowed one of them to catch you..." Her dark red eyes scanned the room pointedly, lingering on the open door to his bedchamber. "I suppose you did not."

"I did not," he confirmed, setting his apple core aside and lifting the tea cup to his lips.

"Mother would be disappointed," she said wistfully, but with no real shame. They were both children who had defied their mother often.

"Mother is not around anymore."

"Indeed. And, in truth, perhaps it is a good thing you did not allow any to catch you. It is, after all, only the first night of The Summit. You still have time to filter out a good mate."

"And if I don't find one?"

Her gaze slid back to him, irises dark but flashing crimson in the afternoon light. She looked him over steadily. "If you don't ...?"

"If I don't find anyone worthy enough to be my mate." He clarified. "If I don't want any of them ...?"

She regarded him coolly, one eyebrow quirked. "I will not force a mate on you, if that's what you're concerned about. I am not our mother. While I do believe, it is your duty to mate and breed, I understand the value of being picky and independent." She set her cup down, rising to her feet in a fluid movement that put his own gracefulness to shame. She straightened her skirts and her bodice, rich red fabric hugging her curves in all the right places. "Still..." she said, idly picking at a stray thread. Her tone was chillingly even, emphasizing a warning with just one word. He stiffened automatically, freezing with his cup poised by his lips. He eyed her warily, waiting for her to continue. She waited long enough to stretch the apprehension. "Do be careful that you do not reach too high, dear brother." She caught his gaze then, piercing and firm. The sharp eyes of the brutal leader she was. He felt it like a knife through his chest. "The fall from such a height could be treacherous..."

She gave him a smile that was far too toothy to be pleasant before sweeping out of the room. She didn't look back and left the heavy double doors open to swing shut on their own.

Rajiah stared after her, mouth agape and eyes wide. He set the cup down with shaking fingers, ignoring the rattle as it was placed on the table. Her threat had been clear. She had noticed his playful invitation to Arulean during his flight. Hell, he wouldn't be surprised if she had noticed the direction of the desire in his scent, or Arulean's reaction to it. She was proud and she was vain, but her mind was sharp and clever.

Something twisted unpleasantly in his gut in the wake of her threat, but something else burned in his chest. He clenched his hands into fists, standing on legs that were solid despite his shaking knees. He wasn't shaking from fear; however, he was shaking from the rush of adrenaline. A rush that came with the knowledge that she saw him as a threat.

Which could only mean that he possibly stood a chance.

He stepped out onto the balcony attached to his rooms, resting his hands on the railing and staring out over the valley. The ember burning in his chest lit to a flame. His sister had warned him away, but, despite her threats and her power, her words only made him want it more.

After all, dragons were stubborn and prideful and eager to take what they wanted. And he was a dragon through and through.

CHAPTER
SIX

Arulean liked to think of himself as an observant man. He was a firm believer that his ability had helped him get to his seat of power. He knew how to watch people, his people. He knew how to discern their motivations, their goals, their likes and dislikes, all from a distance. He believed that observation was the best way to learn about someone.

This had a very specific reason: he was a dragon king. Because of this, people acted differently around him. It wasn't their fault, and he didn't blame them. They found his presence intimidating, and their actions changed around him to show polite respect, loyalty, or concealed contempt. No one could be open around him unless they were higher on the social ladder or a close friend or family. And while Lyphnia chose to keep herself distant and above her peers, Arulean learned how to get glimpses into their lives from afar.

When not in direct interaction, he could see how people acted on their own, their open honesty. He could see their true colors. He could watch how they molded themselves depending on who they interacted with. He could see how his people truly lived, what they truly thought, and what they truly wanted.

So he enjoyed standing off to the side. And while Lyphnia did so, peering out over their kind with a sharp eye, enjoying how they were separated from the rest, he stood, quiet and observant. He watched over his people with a keen eye, not to look down on them, but to watch. Silently watching. Silently determining what he needed to do to help them, to ensure their future, to care for them. His life was one destined to live apart from them. At first, it had seemed like a blessing, but now he saw it as a curse. He felt nothing but loneliness in the distance that separated him from the rest of his people, though he knew it was necessary.

He saw many things. He saw the shyness of attraction, watched it morph into the tentative affection of lovers to the brash boldness of mates. He watched love come and go. He watched tension arise between mates. He watched mateships break. He saw jealousy and acceptance. He saw people take on additional mates, saw tension in some pairings and easiness in others. He watched the rare child play and grow, innocence odd and comforting. He saw the wonder of the world through their eyes. He saw the gruff hardness of the older dragons, saw the shadows in their eyes and the ghost of smiles when they looked upon the young, a touch of sadness lingering on their features. He saw parents, proud. He saw friends, the easy honesty between them, bonds formed for life. He saw friendships break. He saw new ones form.

He watched gossip spread through crowds like a tangible thread. Watched words pass from person to person, saw glances, saw the looks on their faces, saw scandal and interest, amusement and the odd glee that comes from the misfortune of others. He saw it then spread to others, saw the thread twist and twine between individuals until the entire crowd was wrapped in a web. Saw more gossip start, watched more information spread. The source was never definable, but he saw the aftermath, watch the ripples of words through his people.

He perceived the stiffness of politics. Saw when people were tense and polite and when they were relaxed and open. It was easy to discern who liked whom and who set who on edge. He could see who had secret agendas, who were crafty and cunning and careful getting what they wanted. It was easy for him to see Lyphnia's loyal servants moving through the crowd, to see who was easily affected by her sweet word and bold promises.

Mostly, it was easy for him to see the true colors of his people, and it was something he admired greatly. He loved watching interactions between friends and family and lovers. It was something they never exhibited when around him. He set people on edge simply by being who he was.

At least, that was the case for most. There were a few who treated him as an equal. And if not an equal, then at least like a friend. His brother, Gerrald, was one of them. His other siblings, those he had left, saw him as little more than a stranger. Even the few children he had living placed him at a distance, though he wondered how much of that was because of him and how much was their desire to avoid their mother. The Elders had always treated him with respect, but also with blunt honesty, and he had appreciated that.

He'd had more close friends in his youth and at the height of his power. He'd had an entire circle of trusted friends that had been more like family. He would have trusted them with his life, and he had. Just as they had trusted him. There weren't many of them around anymore, and those who were left had drifted away from him. He didn't blame them. After the Purge, after Lyphnia's last rebellion, after she had gone and locked herself away to leave him to grieve for their children and their people alone, he hadn't been the same. He had distanced himself from dragon-kind, and that distance had never gone away. Only Gerrald remained of their once numerous friends.

Him and Lyphnia. Lyphnia, who had been strong and beautiful in her youth. Cunning and clever. She was desirable, and she knew it. She used it to her advantage. She held herself high above all possible mates, eyes set solely on Arulean. And he had fallen for her. She was the only one, of all possible mates, who seemed worthy of him. She worked for his attention without seeming to work at all. She seduced him, and he came willingly. Together they rose in power. Together they were invincible. They ruled their people with a combined iron fist and a passion that sparked through the ages. They were happy, and he was far too young and naive to see her for who she truly was. Far too blind with himself and his own pride to see that she never truly loved him, but the idea of him. That she craved him because of his station and had he been anyone else, she never would have come to his side. He had been too foolish and hungry for more to realize that he was the same way with her.

They were happy, and passionate, and once they had been in love. But it was never for the right reasons.

He had never expected to find someone else who treated him as an equal. Not in this day and age. Not after everything that had happened.

He had never expected Rajiah Bronze.

The man was a complete anomaly. Arulean found himself observing him more and more frequently the longer he stayed in the valley. What originally started as mild curiosity was quickly changing into something deeper. An interest. An interest that was slowly consuming him. An interest that he didn't want to name for fear of falling even deeper.

He watched Rajiah whenever the omega was near. He watched him at festivities, at gatherings. Watched how he interacted with others. For while others seemed more at ease outside of his immediate presence, Rajiah was the opposite. He seemed tenser around crowds of their own kind. Even while he smiled and chatted politely, there was a stiffness about him, something that was holding him distant, a tenseness that spoke volumes for how uncomfortable he felt. He wasn't sure others saw it, but for one as attuned to observing as Arulean was, he saw it clearly. He watched as Rajiah would glance around, eyes always on a method of escape, watched as the young man took it, watched as he slipped away unnoticed by all but Arulean.

And he noticed how Rajiah didn't seem tense when it was just the two of them. It was strange. A one-on-one interaction with nearly anyone always made the other party tense, but not Rajiah. The bronze dragon wasn't afraid to scoff at him, mock him, tease him, or to call him out. He wasn't afraid to voice his opinions. He never backed down from Arulean's powerful alpha presence. Not even when they first met. He was always standing strong and firm, meeting his gaze steadily where others would have looked away.

He wasn't afraid of him, and that was a novelty that Arulean wasn't used to.

He found himself drawn to it, intrigued, unable to pull himself away. Unable to check himself.

"He's an interesting lad, isn't he?" Came a deep, gruff voice, close to his ear.

Arulean was internally startled, but outwardly he barely flinched. He blinked, realizing he had been watching Rajiah again. They were still seated at the head table, but Lyphnia had dragged her brother down into the crowd to mingle. The two of them were currently surrounded by a small group of higher-ranking alphas, all of whom had thirsty eyes for the unmated omega, but were giving their attention respectfully to the queen. Rajiah was undeniably trying to hide behind her.

He tore his eyes away, glancing sidelong at his own brother. The man was giving Arulean a knowing look, waggling both eyebrows as his lips pulled up into a small smirk.

Arulean held his face firmly neutral. "I cannot deny that he is, indeed, interesting." He said carefully, lifting his goblet to his lips to sip his wine.

Gerrald snorted, leaning back in his seat, legs sprawled beneath the table, leaning heavily on one arm of the chair to talk in low tones to Arulean, too quiet for others to overhear even with shifter hearing. "You can't fool me, Arulean. I know just how interesting you think he is."

Arulean raised both brows, trying for nonchalance. "Do you now?"

His brother's grin only widened as he tilted his chin down, gazing up at him with a sparkle in his gray eyes. "I saw you during the flight on the first moon. When he was leading a chase. I saw you when he flew past. I saw how you reacted to his scent."

Arulean bristled, setting his goblet down carefully. "Only a fool wouldn't be affected by him in some way. It's simply biology."

A shiver ran through him at the memory, his eyes finding the man in question, lingering on his thick dark hair pulled into a low ponytail at his nape, exposing the slender lines of his neck. It was once again adorned with a plethora of gold jewelry, as were his wrists. Arulean wasn't sure if he had ever seen the man without them.

He found it difficult to explain, but the strength of the memory was undeniable proof: Rajiah's scent had affected him strongly. More than any scent ever had.

During the flight, he had seen Rajiah leading the chase of many alphas, hungry for the omega. He had seen it, and it had caused something dark to fire up in his gut, but he had held his distance. It wasn't his place to interfere, and if the omega wanted to find a mate, that was his choice. But Rajiah had stayed far ahead of them, not letting any of them near and pulling off movements that looked more for a show of power than anything. It reminded him a lot of Lyphnia in her youth, when she was trying to prove she was a worthy mate by showing none of the others were worth her time.

So he had ignored, or at least tried to ignore, the omega shifting through the winds with the trail of alphas behind him. Even though his dragon wanted nothing more than to dive after him, batter away all the others, and take him for himself. The desire had been strong, but Arulean had always been a man of strong will, so he had resisted.

Then Rajiah had playfully circled him, teasing him, urging him to join whether he meant to or not, surrounding Arulean with his scent.

He'd had to physically stop flying to keep himself from diving after him in that moment. His will had nearly snapped. Rajiah's scent was powerful that night. Sweet and alluring and burying itself deep in his senses, making his mind go hazy with lust and desire and nearly pushing his logic away. It had awoken something in him that had long been dormant. An alpha's instinct, his need. It came roaring back with a vengeance and it had been so startling, that Arulean had nearly lost to it.

If he had, the consequences would have been dire. So, he had resisted, but only barely. No one had been brave enough to bring up his moment of weakness. At least not to him. He could see the anger and accusation in Lyphnia's eyes though. He could see it in the way she shielded Rajiah with her own body, steering him away as soon as was acceptable.

He knew that no alpha would blame him, however. All of them, even the happily mated ones who didn't join the chase, couldn't deny that Rajiah had the most alluring omega scent they had encountered in centuries. This was the fate of a child of the Great Mother, he supposed.

Still, it posed an odd question: if his scent was so strong that night, why was it so weak now? The adrenaline from the flight and the chase and the full moon would have made his pheromones stronger, but the difference went beyond reason. It was mind boggling enough that whenever Rajiah was near, Arulean found himself breathing deeply, trying to catch a glimpse of that tantalizing scent that still haunted his mind, echoing ripples of desire throughout his body whenever he recalled it.

Rajiah Bronze was an anomaly, a puzzle, unlike anyone he had ever known, and Arulean found himself indisputably drawn to him. And it was a battle he was starting to lose.

Gerrald only shrugged. "Biology or not, you were intrigued. You still are. I can see it in the way you stare at him."

"I watch all of our people."

"You watch him specifically. More and more as the days go on."

"He is strange. I am only trying to understand his motives."

Gerrald raised both brows, but his smirk stayed in place. "Motives? He has motives now?"

"Everyone has motives. Especially when it comes to me."

"What could his possibly be?"

"He is Lyphnia's brother," He said plaintively, giving Gerrald a look. "I know better than to blindly trust anyone close to her."

"He doesn't really strike me as someone loyal to her though," He said, idly scratching the stubble on his chin.

Arulean frowned. "And you would know because...?"

He shrugged, small smirk playing on his lips as he gazed over the crowd. "I've been watching him, too."

Something in him shifted, a heaviness, thick and black, sliding into his stomach, tightening it as it coiled into his chest. He stiffened just a fraction, fingers stilling on the table top. "Have you?" He asked, voice far too neutral to be pleasant.

Gerrald snorted a short laugh, smile widening as he nudged him with an elbow. "What's the matter, brother? Jealous?"

Arulean forced himself to make a disinterested sound, looking away. He forced his gaze to bypass Rajiah, scanning the crowd instead. He refused to admit his attention was still hyper focused on the spot where he and Lyphnia stood. "Hardly."

Gerrald nodded, suddenly far too serious and far too grave, cluing him into the farce. "Of course, you're loyal to your mate. Your mate whom you shun from your bed and your heart, but refuse to find another."

"You know my reasons, Gerrald."

"I do, but I don't agree with them."

"As you've made clear."

He idly tapped out a rhythm on the arm of his chair, humming thoughtfully. "I haven't had a mate since Terin passed, Elders rest his soul." He said idly, and far too lightly. Arulean knew that Terin had meant the world to his brother. Their bond had been strong. Terin had died in a stress induced miscarriage during the purge that had taken both his life and the baby's. "I've been thinking about finding another. No one could replace Terin, but life is lonely. I could use a companion to share my days and nights." He leaned a little closer, nodding in the direction of Rajiah. "And he's a pretty little thing, isn't he? There's a fire about him. A stubbornness. I'm willing to bet he'd make all sorts of pretty little noises--"

"Enough," Arulean snapped, surprising them both. The black feeling was seething inside him, twisting and coiling and sinking claws into the inside of his ribs, crawling up his throat.

The thought of Rajiah with another alpha, with his brother or anyone else, someone taming that fire, feeling it in the throes of passion, getting to witness his face and body writhing in pleasure, hearing his voice, cracked and hoarse, body damp with sweat and scent glands swollen and sweet-- he didn't like it. He didn't like that thought one bit. He felt a shifting beneath his skin, his inner dragon rising close to the surface in his agitation. He breathed heavily through his nose, trying to calm himself.

"Jealous?" Gerrald asked, clearly amused.

"No."

"I think you just proved otherwise."

"If you want him, you should take him." He said through gritted teeth, feeling the ache in his jaw. His hands curled into tight fists. "Before Lyphnia mates him off to another alpha."

At this, Gerrald snorted again, and when he spoke, his voice was much softer and kinder. "I don't want him, Arulean. I was just trying to prove a point." He reached out then, gently taking Arulean's hand in his own. The light touch of his calloused fingers was startling enough for him to relax his fist. His brother held his hand, palm up, and Arulean stared in surprise at the streaks of red that oozed from the half crescent holes in his palm from his nails. Gerrald grabbed a cloth napkin and gently dabbed away the blood before it could run down his wrist. "I believe my point was proven sufficiently enough." He looked up at Arulean then, lips forming a tight line, eyes hard and unyielding, but open and honest. "You want him." He said bluntly.

Arulean didn't see the point in denying it. Not to his brother, who knew him so well. After that display, Gerrald wouldn't believe him anyway.

Arulean stared down at his hand, closing it gently around the cloth. "It does not matter."

"Of course it does."

"It doesn't." He repeated, eyes automatically searching for Rajiah again, only to find him missing from Lyphnia's side. He caught sight of him just as he slipped out a door, silent and fleeting as the wind. "I cannot allow myself this." He said softly.

Gerrald made a noise in the back of his throat, indicating just how much he disagreed with that statement.

Gerrald's words haunted him for days. Every time he saw Rajiah, he felt a sudden quickening of his heartbeat, a strange fluttering in his chest, and an odd shortness of breath. He found his eyes following the omega's movements, and his own steps subconsciously trailing after him. Even when Gerrald wasn't with him, he could hear his brother's words in his ear, urging him to go after what he wanted, chase his happiness and let the consequences be damned. And he wanted to. Gods, did he want to.

When Gerrald was with him, he would nudge Arulean playfully and smile teasingly as his eyes drifted to the bronze dragon. These antics often had the effect of making heat flood his face in a blush. A blush! He was Arulean Black, the last dragon king appointed by the Elders. He did not blush.

Yet, he found himself giddy as a young alpha whenever he was around Rajiah.

Instead of retreating to his study, he found himself retreating to the library in hopes of crossing his path. They did several times, and each time he teased Rajiah about avoiding others only to be teased in return. It was an odd familiarity, a comfortable back and forth they developed. He cherished it. It was refreshing and new. Rajiah grew used to him quickly, and any odd tension melted away from their interactions. He showed Rajiah around the library sharing his favorite volumes and digging up ones he hadn't seen in years in hopes they would interest him.

They talked more than read on these occasions, but when they did read, the silence was comfortable and cozy.

Whenever they crossed paths and Lyphnia was around, she would hurry Rajiah away on one errand, excuse or another. Or simply put herself between them. It was in those times where she got more tactile than she had in years, touching his arm, caressing his shoulder as she passed. It took everything in him not to pull away from her touch.

Lyphnia couldn't be with him all the time, however, and Rajiah was a master of sneaking away from others. And Arulean was a master at finding him and running into him as casually as he could.

At feasts and group festivities, they often made eye contact, and Rajiah would make faces at him while one dragon or another droned on and on about something unimportant. Arulean had never found it so hard to keep a straight face. Rajiah took to hovering near him, finding him to be a better deterrent for unwelcome alpha advances than his sister. He didn't mind. He would rather no one approach him with mateship in mind.

It didn't take long for him to feel oddly protective over the omega, despite not having a claim to him. He glared down some of the more persistent and touchy alphas, and there were a few times he distracted a few before sending Rajiah a small wink or a subtle hand gesture to urge him to slip away. The small, thankful smile Rajiah always sent him was well worth the trouble of being trapped in a dreadfully boring conversation.

When Rajiah visited him, he started sneaking him sweets and chocolates and desserts from the kitchens. He always slid them across a desk or into his hand with a small, mischievous smirk before striding away. Arulean could have gotten them at any point on his own without qualm, but there was something sinfully delicious about receiving them from Rajiah's thieving antics.

He took to showing Rajiah all the secret passages and best ways to move about the castle without being caught. He showed him the quickest paths to take and the ones to avoid.

Their time together was rarely long. The castle and valley were inhabited by several hundred dragons, and he had a Summit to see over. There was always one thing or another to pull him away from Rajiah, and he always went, even though everything in him begged him to stay. Still, he cherished the short moments, the secret smiles, the light and hesitant touches.

Despite all the evidence against him, Arulean was still holding himself back. He kept himself in check. He could see himself falling down a slippery slope, but he hung on. For days he held on. But the tension to his anchor was taut and tenuous, threatening to snap and set him free with every whiff of his scent and every look of those brilliant, amber eyes.

He had spent much of the day in the great hall with Lyphnia, meeting with dragons and listening to grievances. They mediated disputes as was their duty, but he, for the most part, did all the work. He listened to each story, both sides, with an open ear, but a bored mind. The upside to going about his daily life without expression was that he could easily hold his face in check to keep from seeming too disrespectful. Lyphnia, unfortunately, hadn't learned that skill. Nearly everything she felt and thought showed on her face, so she spent much of this time lounging on her throne, looking pained and bored and irritated.

She occasionally put in her ideas and thoughts on matters, but he preferred it when she didn't. Her opinions often differed from his own ruling, and it was better that they appear as a united front, for the sake of their kin. There were a few disputes that they agreed on, those where the dragons in question were utterly clueless and completely idiotic. For the most part, however, she kept her commentary to hushed murmurs, and he was grateful.

Unfortunately, this meant when they were done for the day, he was tired and his mind was aching. He wasn't used to interacting with this many people so often anymore. Much less so his own kind, who were known to be stubborn and arrogant half the time, making these matters that much harder.

He skipped dinner that night, opting instead to have food brought to his study. His only regret was that he wouldn't see Rajiah at the nightly feast or usual gathering after, but the peace and quiet he got once he was alone was well worth it. Besides, he reasoned, he shouldn't be disappointed in not seeing him in the first place. Not that it stopped him from feeling so.

He was flipping through several of the scrolls he had set aside to read, each and every one of them recent news and accounts from the recent spread of humans and the movements of shifters around the continent, when he heard the shouts. The words were muffled, but loud enough to carry. He lifted his head, eyes drifting lazily to the open doors to his balcony. He was about to look away, passing the incident off as something someone else could handle, when he recognized a familiar voice.

Heart rate suddenly picking up, his curiosity was piqued.

He did not admit to himself the speed with which he hurried to the balcony. He stopped when he reached the edge, hands resting on the railing automatically as he leaned past to gaze down. His study balcony loomed high on the castle, overlooking the large, grand steps that led up the hill to the castle's front doors. Halfway up those steps, on a flat break between the steps, was a young man. He was no doubt a shifter, though of what kind, Arulean had no idea. He didn't recognize him. He was dressed in ragged and dirty clothes, no doubt those of a traveler.

He was being held back by two servants of the castle, practically dragged backwards as he struggled in their hold, shouting and raving. Lyphnia stood on the steps above them, arms crossed over her chest and her hip cocked to the side. As usual, she was dressed impeccably, not a hair out of place as she stood in regal, cool beauty. What caught his interest, however, was Rajiah, standing between them and pleading with his sister. They were all shouting, drawing in attention from anyone within earshot.

He didn't think before he was already moving, launching himself over the balcony.

He didn't shift all the way. There wasn't enough room for that, but he had enough experience and control over his shifting to go halfway. His body dropping hard and fast and form obscured as it was engulfed in the smoke that streamed from his skin. He was shadow and smoke shooting down to the steps in a controlled fall.

He shifted back to his human form as he landed lightly on his feet in the middle of it all, smoke dissipating as his skin settled back into place and the beginnings of his scales receded. A controlled half shift was difficult to pull off, most shifters were unable to stop and contain the beast once it started to emerge. But he wasn't a king for nothing, and what he had done not only got him to the commotion sooner, but was also a clear show of power and authority.

The arguing had stopped, everyone staring at him with a wide array of expressions, ranging from surprise to irritation to relief. He stood tall, chin lifted as he lightly clasped his hands behind his back. He gazed at them all, making sure to hold contact with everyone for several moments, establishing control over the situation, before flicking his gaze to Lyphnia.

"What is going on here?"

She gave a half shrug, a small sigh, and gestured to the restrained traveler with a careless hand. "This man is here to complain about traveling woes, as if it is our fault that his party came across trouble on the way through our mountains." She said with a sneer. "I was just sending him on his way."

"He came here to ask for our help!" Rajiah snapped, taking a step forward. His face was contorted into a familiar stubborn rage. It was the same look Arulean had seen the night Rajiah had lured him out of the sky. "There are lives in danger and you're sending them away like they're nothing!"

"They are." She said coldly, eyes locking onto her brother's, face gone deathly still. "We are in the middle of a Summit. We have our own kind to attend to--"

"They are our own kind!"

"They are not! We are dragons. They are wolves."

"They need our help--"

"We are busy--"

"We're doing nothing but sitting on our asses!" Rajiah shouted, thrusting a hand out towards the man. "While his people are in danger. We can help them. There are so many of us in the valley right now. We have all the power in the world to help them!"

"We don't know them."

"It doesn't matter!"

She scoffed, rolling her eyes in a dramatic, dismissive fashion, and Rajiah pushed forward.

"They came to this valley, your valley, for sanctuary and to start a new life! They're in danger, and we can help them." He took another step toward her, thrusting an accusing finger in her direction. "If you think you're so superior, why don't you prove it by helping those below you?"

"I have nothing to prove to lesser shifters." She said icily.

"What is the purpose of being a queen if you won't help the people who bow to you?"

She made an indignant sound, hands shooting to her sides as she took a threatening step forward. He could feel her aura flaring, sparks and embers coming off her in angry waves. Her eyes were like daggers, voice like venom. He knew even the strongest of dragons would wilt before her, forced into submission by instinctual self-preservation. Not Rajiah, however. He stood his ground, his own earthy aura firm and unwavering. Arulean had never seen the two fight, but he had no doubt that was where they were headed.

"The purpose is that I rule my own kin, not some flea bitten, wingless dogs with a lifespan akin to ants--"

"Enough." Arulean said sharply, causing both of their attentions to snap to him. He took several steps forward until he was between them, holding his arms out, hands like a barrier to keep them both rooted in place. He glared between them, waiting until they both backed down enough to give him their full attention. "You two will not quarrel on the front steps of our home." He said firmly, holding each of their gazes until they looked away with huffs of irritation. Then his gaze slid to the other three behind Rajiah. "Release him." He commanded, and the servants did so immediately, shuffling away from the traveler quickly.

The man stumbled, falling to his knees. Arulean let his hands drop to his sides and stepped forward, kneeling in front of the man and offering a hand to help him up. The werewolf looked at it, surprise evident in his features. He gazed up at Arulean, warily searching his eyes. Arulean let his lips tug into the barest of smiles, a small twitch of the lips in hopes of indicating his genuine desire to help. It seemed to work, for the man grasped his forearm and Arulean stood, helping him to his feet.

"Tell me what has happened." He said, trying to keep his voice level and kind, but with the firm authority of his station.

The man shifted his weight from foot to foot, glancing sidelong at Rajiah, who must have given him an encouraging look because he looked back with his face set in grim determination. "I'm traveling with my pack," He said, licking his lips and clearing his throat, voice coming stronger. "We wanted to move to the valley. Some of us have family working in the farms at the eastern fields. We were almost there, moving along the river, but the path was too narrow-- there was a rockslide-- half of our wagons were swept into the water, my people along with them. They're trapped now, and the current is too strong for us to reach them on our own." His voice was coming faster, more frantic, his fidgeting increasing as he nervously glanced to the east. "I shifted and ran here as quickly as I could, hoping I could find help..." The look he shot Lyphnia said very plainly what had happened when he got to the castle and what he thought of that.

"How long ago?"

"I--"He hesitated, chewing his bottom lip. "I don't know."

"Are they still alive?" The question was blunt. He realized that when the man flinched. But it had to be asked.

He steeled himself. "They have to be." He said, then softer. "They have to be... There's not much of us left. We were hunted by the humans--"

"We're wasting time!" Rajiah snapped, and Arulean looked at him, eyebrow raised. His face was contorted in anger. Much to Arulean's amused horror, he was already stripping. He untied the sash from his waist, letting it drop before pulling his tunic over his head and dropping it on top. "They need help. Now." He bent to unlace his boots with swift, sure fingers, kicking them off. He stood, glaring at his sister. "And if you," His eyes slid to Arulean. "Won't help, then I will." Hooking his thumbs into the waistband of his pants, he threw them down, stepping out of them.

Arulean felt his heart lodge in his throat, and his body still. He kept his eyes carefully on Rajiah's face. The pounding of his heart was deafening in his ears, his inner dragon rearing his head with interest at the sight of Rajiah's bare body. He breathed heavily and steadily through his nose, willing his own pheromones to keep from acting up. He wasn't used to having to control himself like this.

"Rajiah, don't be rash." Lyphnia was saying with the same stern voice she had used when keeping their children from acting out. It always stopped them in their tracks, but not Rajiah. The omega was pulling off his bracelets, dropping them to his stack of clothes as he glared at her.

"I'm not being rash. I'm being reasonable. They need help. Now. And I'm the only one willing to help them. So I will." He pulled his necklaces over his head, and they dropped to the pile with a sense of finality. The wind brought the omega's scent to Arulean's nose, tickling his senses. It wasn't as strong as the night of the full moon, but now that he was bare, it was certainly stronger than normal.

He kept his feet firmly planted and curled his hands into fists to keep from reaching out.

Rajiah turned to the shifter, who was watching him with hope lighting his features. "Lead me to them. Now."

The werewolf hesitated for only a moment before he was stripping down with practiced speed, tossing his clothes into a bag he had strapped to his back. He shifted quickly, picking up the bag in his teeth before regarding Rajiah. The omega nodded, lips pursed into a determined line. He nodded, and the wolf took off down the steps. Rajiah cast one last scalding look at Lyphnia before shooting Arulean a more reproachful one. His eyes saying more than words could. Then he was running, leaping, and shifting mid air. His scaled body twisted in the air, wings flapping furiously to gain air as he followed the direction of the wolf down below as he weaved through the village.

"He is a fool." Lyphnia's voice broke the silence. He glanced at her, watching the way her lips contorted into distaste, delicate nose crinkling, brows furrowing. Her eyes narrowed on

Rajiah's distant form. "He needs to learn that we must look out for ourselves first and foremost. We cannot help everyone, and they should not expect us to-- what are you doing?"

Arulean already had his shirt off, tossed into the pile with Rajiah's clothes. He rolled his shoulders, feeling the muscles in his back shift and stretch in anticipation of the shift. Pin thin bones of his wings pressing to the surface of his skin, eager to expand, grow, stretch. The pain was pleasant. He kicked off his boots, removing his pants with practiced ease. He tossed away all his adornments, all the things he wore to look like a king of his station.

When he looked back to Lyphnia, he was bare, standing tall and regal even in the nude. The wind was crisp against his pale skin, but the fading rays from the sun were warm.

She was staring at him, lips parted, eyebrows raised a look of absolutely incredulousness adorning her features. He met her gaze steadily, not bothering to plead with her for understanding. He knew it would take a lot of conversation and convincing that they didn't have time for.

"I am doing what needs to be done." He said simply.

"Don't be a fool, Arulean." She said, voice full of warning. It had long since lost its potency with him.

"A fool is one who does not change."

"If we help them now, they will always expect our help. We must look out for ourselves first and foremost." She slid down the stairs and to his side on graceful steps, moving like liquid fire. That fire had once lit something inside him, but now it just felt cold. "Rajiah is still young. He is idealistic in ways that are far too fantastical for reality." Her voice was softer now, soothing, honeyed and sweet. She put a hand on his arm, letting her fingers trail over his skin. It was a touch that had once stirred his heart. Now it just made his skin crawl. She looked up at him through her long lashes, her plump red lips tugged up into a small smile. "Don't encourage his mistakes. He will come around. Come back inside with me." He knew that tone, that sugary sweet voice she used when she wanted something of him. It had once worked. Not anymore.

Arulean put a hand on hers, soft and gentle. Her smile widened a fraction, no doubt in victory. But then his fingers tightened around hers and very gently, very slowly, pulled her hand away from his arm. Her smile fell, brows furrowing in a small, confused frown. She searched his eyes, wary. He released her hand and took a step backwards, away from her.

"Arulean..." She said, voice full of warning. "Don't do this."

"If we don't look after those weaker than us, then what good are we?" He said coolly, steadily, repeating the words that had haunted him for weeks.

"We are dragons!" She snapped, fingers curling into fists as she glared. "We are the most powerful creatures in existence!"

"Then it is time we started putting our power to good use. Or else we are no more than beasts."

He saw the beginnings of confusion and rage contorting her features, but he looked away. He took a step, then another, until he was sprinting to the top of the next set of steps and leaping into the air with all the strength his legs possessed. He let his body hang in the air for one breathless, weightless moment before he shifted, smoke curling and coiling, body swirling and expanding, wings snapping out and catching the wind.

And then he flew after Rajiah and the werewolf without another glance back. He knew Lyphnia would not follow, nor did he expect her to.

Rajiah was far ahead of him, having pushed his smaller body to the limit. He was already on the outer reaches of the valley. Arulean hurried after him, following the glinting of his bronze scales in the light of the setting sun. As he flew, he passed over the werewolf sprinting below, realizing that Rajiah had flown ahead, intent on following the river to the east.

He followed the river out of the valley, between the mountains and through a pass. He was out of Arulean's sight, and by the time he reached the pass himself, Rajiah was nowhere to be seen. He reached out with his senses, looking for the familiar, warm aura. He found it readily enough, spying a glint of scales between the trees. Arulean dove after him.

The river was wide, and the current was quick. The paths on either side of it through the mountain pass were thin and crumbling in places. It wasn't the easiest way into the valley, but it was accessible if need be. It certainly wasn't hospitable for a caravan of wagons. He dove down to the river, spreading his wings and gliding along it downstream. It was wide enough that even his massive wingspan didn't cover the entire thing.

He found them moments later. Several wagons were up turned in the river, the bank of the river had crumbled, clearly showing where they had fallen. Some were caught at the edge, a group of shifters desperately trying to haul them back out of the water, but others had been swept away by the current. Four wagons and carts were scattered further down river, two of which were stuck on rocks. Supplies rushed down river, along with several shifters, clutching to wagons, branches, or rocks.

He knew this section of the river. The waters got choppier, rougher with rapids caused by rocks beneath the surface, leading to a waterfall that dipped over a cliff in the mountainsides. He surveyed the scene quickly, eyes calculating and hard with the need for swift action. Rajiah was below, still in dragon form, helping the pack pull the wagons back up to the path on the water's edge. Despite being bigger than the wagon itself, Rajiah was still small and slight for a dragon. Good for speed and quick maneuvers, not so much for strength.

Arulean dove, hovering over one of the wagons caught on a rock, threatening to shatter with the weight of the current. A mother and her two children were huddled inside, staring up at him in shocked awe, mingling with their looks of terror. He lowered himself slowly and precisely, carefully grabbing the wagon with his claws. When he had a good grip, he beat his wings steadily, rising and pulling the wagon from the water.

He was huge, and the wagon, even when waterlogged and full of shifters and supplies, weighed nearly nothing to him. He plucked it easily from the river and carried it back to the path. He set it on a wider section past where it had crumbled. As soon as it was down, he turned and dove again, going back for another. He finished pulling out another and setting it on the path when Rajiah finished helping them pull the nearly downed wagons back up from the water's edge.

He was far too small to help with the actual lifting of a wagon, so Arulean directed him with a flick of his tail and a nod of his head to the shifters who were holding on for dear life to keep from being swept away in the current. Rajiah hurried towards them without hesitation, plucking soaked men, women, and children from the rushing water. Arulean continued to pull the wagons from the river. It was oddly grueling work. They weighed nothing, but lifting in his dragon form was something he wasn't used to doing. It used muscles that had been dormant for years. He also had to be careful that his grip was on places where the wagon wouldn't fall apart, and carry it in such a way that none of the contents, supplies or people, fell out.

When all was said and done, he joined Rajiah in plucking shifters from the waters, swooping down and hovering to let them cling to his massive forearm before he closed his claws gently around them. When all the people were gone, they started plucking supplies from the water. It became a game of swift dives and sharp eyes. They wove around each other, darting for anything that bobbed in the water. They caught things stopped up on obstacles, snatched things out of the water before they reached the falls, dove beneath the waves to grab things that were sinking.

It all happened so quickly, both of them moving with swift efficiency. Just when he thought they were nearly finished, shouting reached his ears. He whirled his head around, finding the mass of the shifter pack on the shore. They were shouting, words lost in the roar of water and the falls. They were pointing frantically, gesturing. He followed their move-ments, seeing nothing in particular--

There. A child, bobbing in the water, half sinking and hands flailing desperately as they charged down toward the falls. They were too late, too close. Something in Arulean's chest squeezed, leaving him breathless, making him hesitate. Memories of his own children flashed past his mind's eye, their bodies bloody and broken, holding them through their last breaths, having ashes brought to him long after their deaths, bringing those ashes to the burial chamber.

His panic induced trance was shattered as a bronze blur whirled past him, diving over the edge of the falls just seconds after the child. Arulean shook himself, flying over to the falls. He watched from above as Rajiah caught the child, tucking his wings to his sides and curling his body around them just as they hit the water below.

His panic spiked again when Rajiah didn't resurface. And when he did, he was quickly pushed back under by the sheer force of the waterfall. The undertow was strong, dragging him down. He saw him flail, splutter for breath before being pushed back.

Arulean was diving. He tucked his wings in and shot downwards, a black spear cutting into the water below. He was bigger, more able to handle the force of the water. He wrapped his arms around the smaller dragon, used his legs to push off the riverbed. His wings cut into the air, and he struggled hard, but slowly they gained air. He breathed heavily, heart pounding, water rushing off his scales in waves, wings pumping furiously. Rajiah was much heavier than the wagons, but he refused to let go. The bronze dragon remained coiled around the small body of the child, rumbling soft reassurances deep in his throat.

Somehow, they made it back to the pack, though Arulean didn't remember much of it. By the time they landed, he was exhausted. He set Rajiah down gently, who uncurled from the child. They both shifted and the pack rushed forward to thank them. They were both wrapped up in thick, woolen blankets, patted on the back and hugged more times than he could count. Their faces, tear stained but grinning, were overwhelming. He more or less stood there, letting everything wash over him, letting Rajiah tug him around the pack and do the talking for him, while he attempted to simply take it all in. Children clung to his legs, giggling and playing around his feet, not at all afraid of him as their parents were.

"You're smiling." Rajiah said some time later. He had been standing off to the side, watching the pack regather their things and dry them off, preparing to set out once again. The omega snuck up to his side, startling him.

He blinked down at him, momentarily dazed by his brilliant grin. "Am I?" He could vaguely feel the ache in his cheeks.

"You are," He said with a small nod, crossing his arms over his chest as he stood next to Arulean, gazing out over the pack.

"Imagine that..." Arulean said, almost wistfully, voice a murmur. Then louder, "Did we manage to save everyone?"

"We did. They lost some supplies and things, but everyone is safe." He said with a relieved sigh.

"I'm glad."

"Me too..." He was quiet for a moment before speaking again. "Thank you."

"You have nothing to thank me for."

"Thank you for standing by me."

"A wise man once told me that it is our duty as dragons to help those beneath us, that we must look out for all of shifter-kind." He eyed Rajiah sidelong, a smirk playing at his lips. "I was merely doing my duty."

Rajiah grinned at him, looking away, but not before Arulean saw the flush on his cheeks. His scent was much stronger now, though in the wake of their adrenaline-fueled rescue, he didn't feel the draw like he had before. It wasn't a sharp tug, urging him to grab the omega and claim him roughly and quickly. It was a calmer tug, urging him to be merely near him, basking in his warmth and presence, looming over him protectively but not actively.

Looking at the werewolf pack, knowing that they were safe because of him, surrounded by Rajiah's warm, comforting scent, standing by his side, Arulean felt content and at peace. He had forgotten what this felt like.

"Lyphnia won't be happy that you followed me..." Rajiah said offhandedly, cautiously, like he was toeing ice to see if it would hold.

He shrugged. "She wasn't happy when I left, and I don't expect that to change." He hummed idly. "It has been a long time since she has been happy with me. The point is I did what I thought was right, and I will not let her fault me in that."

Rajiah touched him then, a gentle hand on his arm, a brush of his fingers. It was like lightning sparking across his flesh, spreading warmth and drawing him in. His chest fluttered, heat pooling low as his heart picked up speed. It was an instant and uncontrollable reaction. It was a very dangerous reaction. It was one he shouldn't have, but couldn't deny that he did.

"Thank you for coming." He said very, very softly.

"I have a feeling you knew that I would." Arulean said, a teasing tone keeping his voice light despite how heavy that touch made him feel.

Rajiah shrugged, hand dropping. Arulean mourned its loss.

The omega's lips quirked into a small smirk. "I had hoped, but I wasn't sure."

The pack leaders approached them then, issuing more thanks and attempting to give them gifts. Arulean politely declined, telling them to keep what they had and welcoming them to the valley. The wolf who had been a messenger clasped his forearm, locking eyes and thanking him with open honesty and voice thick with emotion. Arulean could do little more than nod, giving his arm a light squeeze. It took a lot of maneuvering to pull themselves away from the pack, but they did so, shedding the blankets and stepping into an open space to shift.

"Race you back?" Rajiah said, amber eyes dancing mischievously, lips quirking up into a small smirk.

Arulean found himself smiling in response, eyebrows raising. "Do you honestly believe you can outfly me?"

"I know I can."

"We shall see about that."

Before he could do anything, however, Rajiah charged him, throwing himself at Arulean and knocking them both to the ground. Arulean was dazed, both from surprise and from the sudden warm sensation of Rajiah's bare body pressed flush against his own. He breathed sharply through his nose as heat shot downwards, his cock twitching eagerly in response. But Rajiah was already scrambling upward, climbing over him and running for the edge of the cliff down to the river.

Arulean realized too late what had happened. He propped himself up on his hands, twisting around to watch the omega run, caught between glaring indignantly and openly staring at his ass. "That is cheating!" He called out, but the only response he got was echoing laughter as Rajiah leapt into the air, shifting, and flying back toward the valley.

Arulean took a moment to simply admire him, cheeks aching, before he pushed himself to his feet and gave chase.

Rajiah had a tendency to be bold and brash and stubborn, but he was not stupid. He knew how to read people and how to read situations, and he knew how to place himself out of harm's way when he needed to. And in this case, that meant avoiding his sister.

Disobeying her wishes and helping lesser shifters? She wouldn't be that surprised. But doing so and inadvertently turning her mate against her? Yeah, she would be mad about that. It wasn't even that he had turned Arulean against her. Arulean had a mind of his own and, while he seemed to be confused over priorities and constantly torn about dragon kin, he was a kind man at heart. He helped people. It wasn't Rajiah's fault that he brought out that quality in him.

If anything, Lyphnia should blame herself for causing enough of a commotion to bring it to Arulean's attention to begin with. He was willing to bet the dragon king would have done the same thing even if Rajiah hadn't been there.

That, of course, was not likely something Lyphnia had considered, and he wasn't about to point it out to her. He'd dealt with his sister's anger plenty of times in the past. If he avoided her long enough, the heat from it would fade and he would only have to deal with the passive aggressive fallout. She was much like their mother in that way.

He wanted to hide in the library, and he knew that part of that was because he always seemed to meet Arulean there. It was like their own little place, a separate space from the castle, where few ever intruded. Still, he knew that Lyphnia knew of his frequent visits to the library, and he knew that she knew that he met Arulean there. For both of their sakes, he decided it would be best if they waited out the brunt of her anger apart. No doubt seeing them together would simply rile her up all over again.

So he stayed away, even though everything in him wanted to be close to the black dragon.

The morning after the incident with the wolf pack, Rajiah woke early. Lyphnia had gotten into the habit of cornering him in his rooms in the mornings either to issue thinly veiled threats, gossip about possible mates for him, or, on occasion, simply enjoy their time together as siblings with a content atmosphere. He knew if she came this morning, it would be to issue threats, and he really wasn't in the mood to deal with a confrontation. So he woke himself with the dawn, dressed, and snuck down to the kitchen to grab some food before heading out to the valley.

He spent the day in the village and the surrounding fields. He visited the tiger pack he had come with, making sure they were settling into the valley all right. He let Regge and Marli drag him around town, showing him their favorite spots and the things they'd seen. They seemed much happier, all of them did. Happier and more at peace, and less tired and ragged and worn as they had on the road.

Once he left them, he traveled out to the eastern fields to make sure the wolf pack had found their way in safely and were settling in. They were grateful to see him and invited him to stay for lunch. He chatted with them, helped them move supplies around the farm, and listened to tales of their travels. They asked him about the black dragon from the previous night, and he told them all about the dragon king, aware of how his cheeks flushed and shy excitement bubbled in his gut along with a burning affection. The wolves listened to him with knowing eyes, but said nothing, for which he was glad.

He made it back to the castle just after the nightly feast began, as was his plan. He didn't want to attend anyway. The idea of sitting in a seat next to a fuming Lyphnia as she acted like a raging, physical barrier between him and Arulean, while annoying them both was not exactly a pleasant one. He figured dealing with any sort of disappointment at his edict was a lesser of two evils.

Instead, he snuck through the kitchens. The cooks there recognized him now, had grown to know him over the past few weeks, and he liked to think they liked him. They were wary of him at first, eyeing him with distaste when he entered the kitchens but holding their tongues. No doubt due to other entitled dragons who came through in search of food at odd times. It didn't take them long to relax around him, however. He seemed to have that effect on shifters. He treated them as equals, and they, in turn, treated him the same. So he was scolded as he came through, hands playfully but firmly slapped as he reached for things, and eventually was able to plead for a knapsack of food. They sent him on his way with a slap on the rump and a fond smile.

He snuck through the hallways as Arulean had showed him, keeping to the lesser used ones. Not that he thought he'd run into many dragons. Most of them should be at the feast. It was the only meal that was served precisely at the same time every day and also served as a social function and essential part of The Summit. He slunk through the halls, climbing the stairs on silent feet.

When he reached an open balcony from one of the halls, he stepped out, gripping the knapsack between his teeth and set to climbing. With skillful, practiced ease, he climbed up the outer stone walls and across the roof, claiming a seat with his back pressed to a tower, a flat section of tiles beneath him, and a picture-perfect view of the valley below.

He was halfway through his meal, enjoying the silence and peace of the night, when a large, dark shadow blocked out the stars.

His heart stuttered in his chest, breath hitching as the dark scaled dragon circled the roof he was on once, twice, and then dissolved into a spear of smoke that drifted down to the slopped shingles. He watched, heart pounding and skin tingling, stomach flipping and heat coursing through his veins.

Only for all of that to dissolve into sour disappointment as Gerrald Onyx stood before him.

The man was grinning, hands on his hips. "What's with the long face?" He teased. "Expecting someone else?"

Rajiah couldn't help the frown that curved his lips. He scoffed, looking away as he ripped off another chunk of bread and stuffed it in his mouth. "I wasn't expecting anyone." He grumbled.

Gerrald chuckled, stepping over to where he sat. "Fair enough. Mind if I join you?"

Rajiah shrugged, disappointment making it increasingly difficult to be polite. Gerrald sat next to him, a respectable distance away, and Rajiah wordlessly handed him the travel cloak he had been wearing from when he visited town.

Gerrald took it with a muttered thanks and wrapped it around his naked form.

They were silent for several long moments. Rajiah wasn't sure what to say, and deny it as he might, he was disappointed, and that was a sour feeling deep in his gut. He had never really interacted with Gerrald Onyx. He'd only seen him from afar and possibly exchanged pleasantries. He hadn't thought the man, despite being an unattached alpha, had any interest in him. He certainly didn't hover over him as many of the other alphas did. Then again, perhaps he was wrong...

Suddenly, the man chuckled. The sound was low, deep, and highly amused. It made Rajiah stiffen, eyeing him sideways warily. "You can relax." He said, tilting his head back against the stone wall behind them, turned slightly to glance at Rajiah. His lips were pulled up into a small smirk. "I'm not here to court you, if that's what you're worried about."

"You're not?" He asked after a moment, cautious as he eyed him curiously. Not that he wasn't happy about it, but it was just... odd. He didn't see any other reason for an alpha like Gerrald to seek him out and sit with him, alone, on the castle's roof, if not to attempt to court him. It wasn't like they were friends, and Rajiah didn't see any other logical reason for them to be friends.

Gerrald chuckled again, shaking his head. He turned his eyes back to the night sky. "No," He said easily. "Not that you're not a lovely omega and any alpha would be lucky to have you," He continued quickly, as if trying to pacify an ego that Rajiah didn't have. "But I'm fairly certain my brother would kill me if I tried. And I don't know about you, but I, for one, do not want to be on the bad side of Arulean Black."

Rajiah stiffened at that, a fluttering of butterflies coming to life in his stomach, rising to his chest and lodging his heart in his throat. "He has no say in the matter." Rajiah said, trying to sound reasonable and keep his voice even. He wasn't sure it worked.

Gerrald eyed him for a moment, eyebrow raised and lips twisting in thought. "No?" He looked away, shrugging. "No, I suppose not. Not if he continues as he has been."

Rajiah didn't know what to say to that, so he said nothing. He set his knapsack aside, food unfinished. After a moment, Gerrald continued.

"You weren't at dinner tonight."

"No."

"May I ask why?"

"What does it matter to you?"

He shrugged again, a light smile playing across his lips. "Curious."

"I..." He looked away, out across the dark valley below. "I was busy visiting friends in the valley today. I didn't make it back until after the feast had started." He paused, then found himself speaking again. "And I felt it would be best if I avoided Lyphnia for the time being." He wasn't sure what possessed him to say it, but there was something about Gerrald that put him at ease. Perhaps it was because Arulean trusted him, or perhaps it was because of his own calm aura, but either way, Rajiah found himself trusting him.

"She did seem rather... perturbed today." He said with a pointed pause. "Does this have to do with the event yesterday with the wolf pack?" He sounded like he already knew the answer.

"You know about that?"

"Arulean told me."

Rajiah hummed his acknowledgement. "She gets like this often. I've found the best thing to do is avoid her until the storm has passed."

"Do you regret what you did?"

"What?" Rajiah looked at him, startled.

He kept staring at the sky. "Do you regret what you did?"

"No." He said without hesitation.

He nodded. "I think what the two of you did was a good thing. You helped people. You saved lives. And I think Arulean agrees with me."

Rajiah felt another fluttering at that. "How is he?" He asked, voice just a tad breathless. He hadn't seen or heard from the man all day.

Gerrald shrugged. "He is as he always is, though... there is something changed about him recently. He seems less withdrawn, more firm in his convictions, more firmly rooted in this reality. In the recent years, though he cares, he was known to... pull away. Mentally and emotionally. But these past few weeks, he has been... he seems more alive. Like the man he once was, but whom I haven't seen in many, many years..." Rajiah stayed silent, and Gerrald thoughtfully drummed his fingers on his own knee. Rajiah wasn't sure if he was talking to him anymore, or if he was just speaking out loud, but either way he listened. "He does what he can to control her." Rajiah didn't have to ask to know who he meant. "Her ambitions are dangerous. She's hotheaded and rash. She dragged on the war and the purge far longer than Arulean wanted to, and, because of her, we lost a lot more of our people than we should have. They lost several of their own children." His voice was soft, solemn, thoughtful, and it drew Rajiah in. "It was then that the rift between them became very apparent, and when it was irrevocable. He has grown and changed a lot since his youth, but she has not. If anything, she has gotten more bitter and more angry. She is a loose cannon, and there's no telling when she will blow and start a war that will wipe us out for good." He seemed to pause then, blink, and glance at Rajiah. "No offense?"

He snorted a short, dry laugh, and waved the man off. "None taken. I know how she is, and our personal opinions differ greatly."

A small smile curved his lips at that. "Glad to hear it." He looked away again. "She is unpredictable and dangerous, but the trouble lies in the fact that she is still powerful and influential, and there are still many who would side with her should it come down to it. Arulean does what he can to keep her contained, to control her, but I fear that in the end, she is controlling him." His voice grew sad with edges of bitterness. "He is the chain that keeps her held back, but with every passing year, she wears on him little by little. He retreats into himself, unable to find things that bring him the happiness that make life worth living, and still she lives on, fueled by whatever fire is alive in her. Meanwhile, Arulean's fire slowly suffocates."

Rajiah shifted uncomfortably. He didn't know what to say, and he didn't think this was information that Arulean wanted him to know.

"Why are you telling me this?" He asked softly, almost afraid to hear the answer.

A soft smile was on Gerrald's lips, but he didn't look at him. "You make him happy." He said softly, voice barely above a whisper and filled with genuine awe. "I haven't seen him like this in centuries. It's subtle, I know it is, but trust me when I say that you make him happy. I have missed seeing my brother happy. With everything he has done for our kind, with everything that he continues to do for us, he deserves some happiness in his life."

Rajiah opened his mouth to say something, but closed it when nothing came out. He cleared his throat, scratching the back of his neck as he looked away. "He... is a very good man." He said softly.

"He is, and as a good man, he believes that he cannot pick another mate for fear of loosening the tight chain he has Lyphnia on. Even if it would make him happy."

Rajiah turned to him then, facing him in the moonlight, lips pursed and brows furrowed. "What are you trying to say?" He asked, voice unwavering and firm. Gerrald turned then to look at him, brows raised. Rajiah held his gaze and continued, voice soft but no less firm. "Why are you telling me this?"

Gerrald looked him over for several long moments before speaking. "He will not make the first move." He said, all humor and lightness gone from his voice. "Even if you give him every open opportunity, even if you make your intentions explicitly clear, even if it is something that both of you want, he will not make the first move. If anything is to come of you two, you will have to be the one to do it."

He stood then, handing Rajiah his cloak back. He stretched

his arms high over his head, the muscles of his broad chest and shoulders rolling under his scarred skin. He was a handsome man, everything an alpha should be, and yet Rajiah felt nothing looking at him. Just like he did when he looked at everyone except for Arulean. Arulean, who set his skin ablaze and made his insides churn with want. Gerrald stepped forward to the edge of the roof, pausing as he looked out into the night.

"Why are you telling me this?" Rajiah found himself asking, voice soft but knowing the man would hear him. "Why are you so sure he's what I want?"

Gerrald half turned then, looking at him over his shoulder, a small smirk playing across his lips in the moonlight. "Because I've seen the way you look at him." He said simply. "It's the same way he looks at you."

And with that, he leapt off the roof, shifting in the air and spreading his wings as he glided out over the valley, leaving Rajiah alone with his thoughts.

CHAPTER
SEVEN

Gerald's advice haunted him for the next few days. He thought about his words in his waking hours, dreaming of Arulean while he slept. He thought of them whenever he saw the black dragon, whenever his eyes fell on his tall, regal form in the distance, heart fluttering whenever those stoic lips quirked just a fraction at the sight of him. The words haunted him day and night, consuming his thoughts, and before he even realized what he was doing, he was planning his first move.

He still avoided Arulean for the most part, which had very little to do with the man himself and everything to do with the fact that Lyphnia was hovering around him ever since the incident with the wolf pack. She clung to him more than was strictly necessary. So much so, that Rajiah could see the irritation flickering in Arulean's eyes, tightening the lines at the edges of his mouth. She still came to visit him most mornings, but her demeanor was far too pleasant and innocent to be real. She never brought up Arulean.

As the last remaining dragon king and queen, and the callers of The Summit, they had a lot of responsibilities to attend to. They had to listen to the grievances of their people, they had to attend meetings and ceremonies, and they had to constantly watch out for and direct the dragons living in the valley. Still, Lyphnia was around him a lot more frequently than she had been the previous weeks, and Rajiah wasn't foolish enough to think it wasn't because she was trying to stake her claim.

It wasn't a warning to anyone but him.

So he watched and he waited and he thought. He watched from a safe distance, blending into the shadows and keeping an eye on Arulean as often as he could without drawing too much attention to himself. He waited, learning their patterns, noting when Lyphnia was around and when she wasn't. And he thought. He thought about Arulean, thought about what the best way to approach him would be, and thought about what he would even say or do when he got the chance.

He wanted to blame his hesitance on Lyphnia's hovering, but the truth of the matter was in his nerves. He had plenty of opportunities to find Arulean alone in the days that passed, plenty of opportunities to pull him aside. But every time he got one of those opportunities, he hesitated. Despite Gerald's unwavering confidence, Rajiah was unsure. He knew he wanted Arulean. His entire being called out for him, wanted him, desired him. And on some level, he knew that Arulean wanted him, too. But the man had an unwavering will and determination, and Rajiah wasn't sure if he would be enough to break that. No matter what Gerrald had said.

So, he hesitated, and continued to wait and watch.

He got his opportunity to make the first move a week into The Summit.

A week after the full moon, a gala was scheduled at the castle. It was a more formal occasion than the nightly feasts of The Summit, and dragons came dressed in their best, determined to impress and show off the wealth they had accumulated throughout the years. To Rajiah, they looked like a flock of peacocks, each one trying to look grander than the next.

He, himself, was dressed in silks and satin, rich browns and golds that complemented his skin tone. The style was lavish and complicated, but at least the rich fabric kept the costume from being itchy or uncomfortable. Lyphnia had chosen his garments, insisting that, as her brother and a desirable omega of high standing, he needed to look his best. She attempted to get him to take off his usual scent blocking jewelry in trade for fancier, jewel encrusted gold bands, but he refused. He was already going to stand out, and he didn't want to make that worse by letting his scent be potent.

Lyphnia was the jewel of the gala, as was no doubt her intention. A deep red gown, ruby encrusted jewelry, and a circlet of gold and rubies adorning her forehead. She was the perfect mix of beauty and danger, and she turned heads everywhere she went. Luckily, that meant he could easily slip into her shadow or slip away.

Dinner that night had been held early, and afterward, instead of the usual social gathering, everyone returned to their rooms to prepare for the gala. After she had gotten ready herself, Lyphnia had come to his rooms with servants in tow to help him prepare. No doubt to also keep him from skipping the whole thing altogether.

He knew she wanted him to choose a mate, and she was doing a damn fine job of making him look desirable.

He trailed after her as she led the way to the great hall, which was set and decorated as the center stage for the gala. The great hall was large itself, and had a second-floor balcony to fit more people, and doors to either side that opened up into two large courtyards. As long as no one shifted, it would easily fit the several hundred dragons at The Summit.

Lyphnia had specifically arranged it so she and Arulean would arrive after everyone else as a symbolic show of status.

When they arrived in the hall outside the grand staircase that led down into the great hall, Rajiah's eyes landed and fixed on Arulean. He was dressed in clothes that fit him in all the right places. Black and white, a monochrome that fit his hair, eyes, and skin. He stood outside the doors, adjusting a cuff, face fixed into passive relaxation. He looked perfect, like a painting, surreal and far, far out of Rajiah's reach. But he wanted to touch. Holy hell, did he want to touch. The man was beautiful, handsome, and powerful, and made Rajiah's insides turn to mush.

He looked up as they approached, and when their eyes locked, everyone else in the hall seemed to fade away. He watched as those dark eyes looked him up and down, saw the spark of hunger there that made him stand a little straighter with pride. His lips curled into a small smirk, and he saw it reflected on Arulean's face. The moment was short-lived before Lyphnia stepped up to him and wrapped an arm through Arulean's, but it was a moment, with Arulean's lingering eyes on him, that gave him all the confidence he needed.

Gerrald stepped up to him and offered an arm, which Rajiah gladly took. They shared knowing looks, glancing in Arulean's direction while Lyphnia was distracted, and chuckled at the man's small frown. They stepped through the doors and slowly made their way down the grand staircase into the great hall. Rajiah would be lying if he said he didn't put a little extra sway into his hips knowing that Arulean was watching.

Arulean and Lyphnia made their grand entrance not long after, with a fanfare from the musicians set up on the second-floor balcony and a hush over the crowd. Arulean looked as impassively powerful as ever, while Lyphnia smiled and waved and ate up the attention.

While they made their rounds and the gala officially began, Rajiah found himself sticking close to Gerrald. It was an unspoken agreement that they had both seemed to come to. While holding onto Gerrald's arm, no other alphas approached him to vie for his attention in an attempt at courtship. Instead they waited at the sidelines, watching and waiting for him to be free to strike, all of them, intimidated by an older and stronger alpha like Gerrald Onyx. Meanwhile, Gerrald was glad for Rajiah's company. He found he was relaxed around the alpha, no doubt due to the fact that his intentions had been made clear. Gerrald had an aura of easy calm around him, and Rajiah found himself relaxing with it. He liked the man. They got along well, and spent much of their time whispering about the dragons around them, heads bent together as they snickered.

More times than he could count, he found Arulean's eyes on the two of them, lips pressed into a small frown and brows furrowed. Whenever he saw this, he would nudge Gerrald, and the two of them would smile sweetly and wave.

The jealousy he felt coming off Arulean in waves was oddly refreshing and made him feel powerful.

The gala passed in a blur. He was led around by Gerrald, reveling in Arulean's glances and ignoring Lyphnia's glares. He was pulled into several dances with Gerrald against his will, but he ended up having more fun than he thought he would. The man was flamboyantly energetic, going over-board with the dramatics to make him laugh. It was much less fun when several other alphas asked to cut in and Gerrald couldn't politely refuse. Instead he backed away with an apologetic smile and hovered nearby should he need rescue.

He did manage to get paired up with Arulean for one, brief dance. They spent the entire thing in polite conversation, both of them far, far too aware of Lyphnia dancing nearby, eyes and ears trained on them. But while their words were distant and stiff, their bodies were not. Rajiah leaned into Arulean's touch, which lingered far too long and was far too bold to be strictly respectable. His eyes bore into Rajiah's, dark and glinting with words he dared not say, but which Rajiah heard anyway. On more than one occasion, Rajiah let his fingertips teasingly caress Arulean's body, taking moments to press his hips against Arulean's, brushing their thighs together. He heard the man's breath hitch, felt the way his hands tightened just a fraction, and he reveled in how powerful it made him feel.

They broke apart nearly as soon as the song ended, but their eyes lingered until Gerrald came and swooped him up into the next dance.

The night was late and the moon was high when his chance came.

The festivities were still in full swing, but were easily on the back half of it. People were starting to wander away from the great hall, back toward their rooms and to the courtyards. Several dragons had stripped of their garments and had taken to the skies, creating a muted multicolored moonlit display above the valley. There were still dancers, but many of the dragons had taken to talking and sipping wine rather than dancing, so the musicians played calmer tunes.

Rajiah had spent much of the evening acutely aware of where Arulean was at all times. Everything about the man called out to him, his presence, his voice, his scent. So Rajiah wasn't sure how he had missed him slipping out of the great hall, but he noticed the strangeness left by his absence.

"Do you see Arulean anywhere?" He asked in a low voice, sipping from a goblet as his eyes roamed the great hall, both the bottom floor and the second above them. It was a rhetorical question. He knew without a doubt that the man was no longer in the room.

Gerrald's eyes lazily scanned the area, eyebrows raised as he slowly lowered his own goblet to the table nearby. "No, I don't." He said idly, sounding distracted. Then his gaze went sharper, and Rajiah followed it to where Lyphnia was caught up in a ring of young admirers and older political acquaintances. She didn't seem to notice the missing presence of her mate, or perhaps she simply didn't care. Suddenly, Gerrald was grabbing his goblet, setting it down as he tugged Rajiah by the wrist. "Come on," He hissed, slipping through the crowd with far more dexterity and grace than he would have expected from such a large man.

He led them through one of the courtyard, weaving through people and darting around the hedges. Rajiah followed him, heart pounding in his chest and breath coming in short, quick bursts. Gerrald never let go of Rajiah's wrist, but Rajiah kept pace with him. Several times Gerrald paused, lifting his nose to the wind and inhaling deeply, eyes darting around with the cold, hard precision of a hunter.

He led him through the courtyard and into halls on the other side of the castle. They hurried through the halls, between sections of the castle, and out the other side. The ground sloped away from the castle and into the castle's grand courtyards.

"Why're we here?" He asked when Gerrald paused, eyes scanning the garden before them.

"He's here."

Rajiah's eyes narrowed. "I don't smell him?"

Gerrald looked at him then, eyes dancing with amusement as he smiled. "He knows how to move around the castle and hide himself and his scent. He knows he can never truly hide, what with his presence being so noticeable, but he knows how to make it harder to find him when he wants to be alone."

He tugged Rajiah forward and they entered the gardens through the archway between hedges. The hedges were plentiful and tall enough that not even Arulean could see over the top them. The gardens were almost maze-like, creating pathways and rooms, large square sections of the garden to showcase different flowers and plants and statues and fountains.

"If he doesn't want to be found, should we be here?" Rajiah asked, nerves starting to make him jittery. He glanced around, tried to catch a whiff of Arulean's scent, but all he could smell was the miasma of floral scents.

"You want to be alone with him, don't you?" Rajiah remained silent. "No use denying it. I've seen the way you've watched him all night. Now might be your best chance. Not even Lyphnia comes here when Arulean wants to be alone."

Rajiah pursed his lips. "But she's been very... watchful of him lately."

"Once we find him, I'll go keep an eye on the castle. I'll send a signal if she comes toward the gardens."

"What's the signal?"

"It will be obvious."

"Like what?"

"Like a giant black and gray dragon flying overhead."

Rajiah quirked a small smile. "Fair enough."

They found him shortly after that. Gerrald slowed to a halt, as they approached another of the sectioned off rooms within the hedge maze. He let go of Rajiah's wrist, putting a finger to his lips, and winked before slowly backing away. He gave Rajiah an encouraging smile before turning on his heel and jogging away. Rajiah watched him go before turning back to the path. Breathing deep, he steeled his nerves, tried to calm his fluttering stomach, and stepped forward through the archway.

The small area was sectioned off by four walls of tall hedges, and a stone fountain dark with moss stood in the center. Tall rose bushes rose along the edges, mixing with the hedges and creating a floral atmosphere. There was a stone bench on the far side, but Arulean sat on the lip of the fountain, his back to Rajiah. His head was tilted downward, his fingers idly trailing in slow, indiscernible patterns in the water.

Rajiah paused just inside the archway, feeling as if he were entering a space separated from reality, a private place where he wasn't welcome. But Gerrald's words were echoing in his mind, giving him the courage he needed to step deeper into the garden section, towards Arulean. The man looked so serene and at peace, much more so than he ever did while in the castle. Rajiah was almost afraid to shatter the moment, but at the same time he was driven forward with the desire to touch, to feel, to hold.

He barely dared to breathe, stepping forward with silent steps on the worn cobblestone.

Here confined in the small area, hedge walls blocking out everything from the world except the night sky, he could finally smell Arulean's scent. It was strong and powerful, smelling of cold damp earth and the salt of man. It made something in him rise to the surface, a hungry desire that made him feel like a predator stalking his prey. His movements became more languid. He felt it in the way he walked, each step measured and careful. His fingers itched to reach out, but he kept them loose at his sides.

The wind shifted. He felt the breeze rustle the stray strands that had fallen from his ponytail and tickle his neck, brushing past his scent glands and carrying his scent forward. He saw the moment it reached Arulean. Saw the way the man's back stiffened, his hand stilling in the water.

"What are you doing here?" He asked, voice carefully neutral and giving nothing away. It stopped Rajiah in his tracks.

He swallowed past the lump in his throat. "Why wouldn't I be here?" He shot back, doing his best to mimic Arulean's tone.

"You seemed to be enjoying yourself with Gerrald." This time his passive voice seemed to crack a little, leaking out some of the bitterness he couldn't quite hide.

Rajiah couldn't help the amused quirk on his lips, or how it bled into his voice. "Gerrald is the one who led me here." He said, slowly taking another step forward, and then another. "I wouldn't have been able to find you otherwise." Arulean turned his head then, gazing at Rajiah over his shoulder with steady, calculating dark eyes. "Right now, he's keeping a watch over the gardens. He said he'll give us a signal if Lyphnia comes."

Something shifted in Arulean's eyes, and it sent shivers down his spine. His gaze was far too intense, and he found himself looking away, gazing into the water of the fountain. He stepped up to the stone lip, opposite side from Arulean. He bent down to touch the curved edge with his fingertips.

"Is he now?" Arulean said, filling the silence with more neutral words.

Rajiah took a slow step around the edge of the fountain, trailing his fingers along the stone, enjoying the rough texture. He nodded, keeping his eyes on the water as he said conversationally, "Your brother makes a good shield." He gave Arulean a chance to respond, but he didn't, so Rajiah kept going. He took another step, dragging his feet with tantalizing slowness. "I kept him company and entertained, and his presence keeps the suitors away from me. So few dared to approach me with Gerrald Onyx on my arm. It was very liberating." Another step, fingers dragging against stone. He kept his eyes on the water but lifted his chin, exposing the long line of his neck. The shift in Arulean's scent was almost instant, and he could have sworn he heard a low rumbling in his throat. "Your brother is a very charming person, very unlike the other alphas I've met in my time here. He's someone I actually enjoy the company of..."

"If you enjoy his company so much," Arulean said, a frigid bite accompanying each word. The bitterness was more apparent, an underlying anger that was probably meant to push him away, but only succeeded in drawing him closer. Jealousy was not a good color on Arulean Black, but Rajiah was enjoying it immensely. "Why don't you choose him? He is unmated and a very eligible alpha."

Rajiah hummed, strides unwavering as he walked around the fountain. Arulean didn't budge from where he was sat upon the lip. His eyes never left Rajiah. "True," He said thoughtfully, putting some sway in his hips as he walked. "It would be very easy to choose him. He's kind," A step closer. "He's strong," He lifted his gaze to meet Arulean's, looking up at him through his lashes. "He's powerful," Arulean's gaze was hard, lips pursed into a small frown. Rajiah didn't waver. He stepped closer. "He's of a good lineage." He lifted his fingertips from the stone of the fountain. "No one would protest our union. Not even Lyphnia could stand against us." He stepped up in front of Arulean, finally stopping as he turned to face him. "There's only one problem..."

Arulean rested his hands on the stone lip on either side of him, head tilted back a fraction in order to hold his gaze. His expression remained stony, his posture stiff, but he didn't protest and didn't move away as Rajiah took a step forward, putting himself between the man's knees. Rajiah paused then, letting the breeze caress his heated flesh, letting it fill his nose with Arulean's alluring scent, thick and strong and drawing him in.

"And what is that?" Arulean asked, voice low and hoarse. At Rajiah's nearness, the bitter jealousy had seeped out of his features, but it was replaced with a new kind of apprehension.

If anything is to come of you two, you will have to be the one to do it.

"I do not want Gerrald Onyx." Rajiah said, voice pitched low as he gazed at Arulean through half-lidded eyes. He could hear the waver in his voice, the scratchiness that came from holding back from the man's powerful scent. His mouth felt very dry. He licked his lips, reveling in the way Arulean's eyes followed the movement. He leaned forward then, slowly, giving the man plenty of time to lean away. He didn't. He held perfectly still, and it was silent enough that he heard the hitch in the man's breath as he held it. Rajiah didn't touch him, but stopped when his lips were right next to his ear, brushing against it with every movement. It was then that he breathed, voice low and honest and strained with need, "I want you, Arulean Black."

This time, he definitely heard a growl coming from the other man. "Rajiah..." He rumbled. His name was both a warning and a plea.

He leaned back, stopping when they were face to face, barely inches apart. Arulean's head was tilted back to look at him, and something primal in him relished in the alpha bearing his neck too vulnerably for him. At this distance, with Arulean's scent so close and strong in his nose, over-whelming his senses, Rajiah could no longer hold back his need to touch. He reached out with a slow but steady hand, running his fingertips along Arulean's shoulder, his collar-bone, up the length of his neck, dancing around his scent glands with playful touches. He felt the man, one of the strongest and most powerful of their kind, shiver beneath his fingertips, and it made something possessive stir within him.

His fingers stopped beneath Arulean's chin, holding him in place while his thumb lightly caressed the man's bottom lip. It was a bold move, and he knew it, but the way Arulean shivered and leaned into the touch, eyes fluttering closed for a moment, only encouraged him.

Rajiah could feel his breath on his lips, coming in long, slow exhales, like he was making a conscious effort to keep it even. He leaned forward a fraction, brushing their noses against one another. The simple touch was electric and extremely intimate. Arulean's eyes shuttered closed.

"Do you want me, Arulean?" He breathed, voice barely above a whisper.

"I..." He was pleased when Arulean's voice cracked. He had barely touched him, and yet he was watching the man crumble before his eyes. "I shouldn't..." He sounded wrecked, heartbroken, and weak. A man with strong resolve about to shatter.

And Rajiah was determined to shatter it thoroughly.

"That's not what I asked..." He said softly, gently rubbing the tip of his nose against Arulean's. He watched him, marveled at his closeness, but Arulean's eyes remained shut. "Do you want me, Arulean?"

"We cannot..." He tried again, licking his lips, tongue brushing against Rajiah's thumb. He shivered, and after a brief hesitation, Arulean did it again, sucking the tip of his thumb between his lips, nipping lightly at it with his teeth and flicking the tip with his tongue. A violent shudder vibrated down his spine, and Arulean's eyes opened then, half-lidded and dark with desire as he held Rajiah's captive. He released his thumb and repeated, "We shouldn't..."

"I don't care." Rajiah pulled his thumb away, stepping half a step closer, until his legs bumped against the stone of the fountain between Arulean's legs. Arulean's hands made their way to his hips, thumbs idly brushing the bones beneath the fabric of his clothes and fingers splayed wide, crawling up to his waist. His hands were warm and large, strong and firm. His grip tightened, but Rajiah wasn't sure if it was to push him away or pull him closer. He didn't move to do either.

Rajiah draped his arms over Arulean's shoulders, fingers trailing through his hair, tugging out the tie to let the strands fall free, combing his fingers through them. Arulean shivered beneath him, and this time when his fingers tightened, it was to pull him closer, arching his body into his chest.

It was all the encouragement Rajiah needed to tilt his chin up a fraction, brushing his bottom lip against Arulean's top lip, a brief and subtle nudge, but so powerful. He pulled away, putting a few inches between them. "Do you want me, Arulean?" He repeated. He ducked forward again, tip of his tongue snaking out to run along Arulean's lips. "Tell me you don't want me, and I'll stop."

Arulean groaned, a low sound, barely a rumble tagged on the end of a long sigh. "Rajiah..." He said again, and Rajiah liked the sound of his name on those lips, ragged and wretched like it had been ripped from his throat against his will.

"Do you want me, Arulean?" He breathed, lightly nibbling on the man's bottom lip. He gave it a tug, letting it go with a small pop. He pulled back a little then, giving them both breathing room. They were both panting, no doubt from a mix of trying to hold back and the eager, silent promise of what was to come. "I'll leave if you tell me to--"

He didn't get to finish the thought.

One of Arulean's hands shot out, fingers digging into the hair at the back of his head, clenching his fist to hold him tight. He yanked Rajiah forward until their lips met in earnest, a low growl rumbling in his throat as his lips eagerly devoured Rajiah's. Rajiah moaned, long and low, opening his mouth eagerly as Arulean's tongue pushed past his lips. His own hands tightened in Arulean's hair, tilting his head so they were at a better angle.

The kiss wasn't gentle, and it wasn't kind. It was a brutal clash of lips and tongue and teeth, both of them sloppy in their eagerness and aggressive in their desperation. It was a clash of two forces, two floods let loose as the dams broke, coming together with enough force to wash them both away. Hands grabbed at his hair, at his hips, his waist, his back, nails digging into his flesh, ripping the fabric of his clothes. The sound of each rip was exhilaration and adrenaline. He growled back against him, refusing to submit and giving as good as he got. His hands roamed, grasping and groping any part of him he could touch. He'd been wanting to touch for so long, and now he couldn't hold back.

Arulean's scent was in his nose, clogging his senses. His taste was on his tongue, dark and alluring, his hands were on his skin, warm and coarse and leaving trails of fire that tingled in their wake.

It was the best kiss he'd ever experienced. It was perfect.

A rustling in the garden broke them apart, both going still and panting for breath as they listened, hands frozen on one another but refusing to let go. Their eyes darted this way and that, trying to track the sound. A night owl flew by overhead, and the two of them relaxed.

Then they looked at each other, and as their eyes met, a wave of calm washed over them, quelling the fire.

Without saying a word, Arulean reached out, gently cupping his cheek. Rajiah leaned into the touch, nuzzling into his palm and playfully nipping at his thumb. A small smile curved the corners of the alpha's lips, face softening as something fond took over his features. He pulled him in again, leaning forward to meet halfway, and Rajiah's breath shuddered out in a soft, eager moan.

This time their kiss was gentle, hesitant but determined. They explored each other's lips and mouths and bodies in a gentle back and forth. Reverent touches and eager bobs of their heads. Rajiah clung to him for dear life, afraid that if he let go, he might float away and never return. Arulean held onto him like he was an anchor and a last breath of air before he drowned.

Time seemed to move like molasses, at a near standstill while they existed in their own little bubble. Together, wrapped in each other's embrace, surrounded by the high hedge walls and the floral scents of the garden, half-hidden from the sky and dragons over head by a canopy of vines and the shadows, they simply indulged in each other. Nearly innocent touches, yet touching with an underlying passion that burned with every movement, sparking when they came together.

By the time a large dragon came swooping low over the garden, startling them apart, Rajiah had been pulled into Arulean's lap, body gently and desperately rocking and grinding against his. He nearly jumped out of Arulean's lap, stumbling to catch his feet under wobbling legs. He caught sight of the dark gray scales as Gerrald's tail went swooping past their field of vision. He ran a hand through his hair, feeling flushed and disoriented but so deeply satisfied, yet still needing more.

He looked back to Arulean, who had already gotten to his feet, pale skin flushed, dark hair mused, thin lips bruised and swollen.

I did that. Rajiah thought, a thrill running through him, heat coiling low in his belly.

"That was the signal." He said, surprised at how breathless he sounded, his voice hoarse with disuse. He no doubt looked as frantic and disoriented as he felt.

Arulean gestured sharply at an archway across from the one he had entered from. "Go," He said, eyes finding more focus and clarity than Rajiah felt he was able to. "If Lyphnia is coming, you won't want her to find you like... this," He said, voice softening. He took a step forward, running his fingertips from Rajiah's temple to jaw, tilting his chin up with gentle fingers. "Smelling of me with those prettily bruised lips..." He said softly, sounded distracted and mostly to himself. Rajiah's toes curled in his boots, body shaking beneath his gentle but firm touch.

"What will you say to her?" Rajiah asked, trying to focus through his need. "You smell like me, too..." And he did, a fact that pleased him greatly.

Arulean threw back his head then and laughed. It was such a deep and surprised sound, one that Rajiah rarely heard but treasured immensely. When he looked back, he was grinning, eyes crinkling at the corners and eyes shining with mirth. It took Rajiah's breath away, and he was pretty sure his heart stuttered to a stop in his chest.

"I will not be meeting with her like this." He said, giving Rajiah a small wink. He felt his brain spark and fizzle, fading to black as it ceased to function. "I'll be running in the opposite direction. She can only catch one of us." He teased, playfulness filling his voice, practically brimming with a joyful high that was so unlike him and yet so beautiful.

I did that. Rajiah's mind repeated. *I made him like this, bruised and mused and happy.*

His own happy warm bubbled in his chest, speaking out

through his limbs as he smirked, tilting his head playfully. "It won't be me she catches, old man."

They darted away from each other, each taking a different archway away from their small meeting spot. Rajiah rushed through the maze-like garden in the opposite direction he had entered from, unsure of where he was going but pushing onward anyway, heart pounding in his chest. He ran, but he felt like he was soaring, the sound of Arulean's laughter echoing in his mind.

CHAPTER
EIGHT

Arulean had always considered himself a patient man. He saw himself as a man of strong will that couldn't be broken. He had always been someone who could and would do what needed to be done. He was a man of duty, dedicated to doing what he must to protect and ensure the future of his kind. He was a dragon king, and he was determined to act like it. He was unwavering, unbending, solid in his decisions and firm in his convictions. Temptation was a drug of his youth that he had long since given up, one that no longer had any power over him. He was a firm foundation on which his kind could stand, one that would weather the storm of Lyphnia, an anchor to keep her from running rampant.

And all it took to tear down that conviction was a willful and beautiful omega by the name of Rajiah Bronze.

"You're glaring..." Gerrald muttered, amusement lacing his tone.

"I am not." Arulean snapped, hands clasped behind his back, standing tall, and very firmly glaring at the mass of alphas surrounding Rajiah across the great hall.

"Mhmmm..." His brother hummed, sipping wine from his goblet, other arm crossed over his chest as he leaned his weight to one hip. "Whatever you say, brother..." He said, nudging Arulean's shoulder with his own.

Arulean ignored the touch. "I have no reason to glare." He insisted, eyes unwavering as he observed them all. They were like vultures, swarming the young and vulnerable. A pack of hyenas prepared to pick off a savory delight. And, damn, if

Rajiah wasn't savory. Savory and sweet and delicious and--
"He can do what he wants." Elders forbid, anyone tell Rajiah
Bronze what to do.

"Who now?"

"What?" Arulean finally tore his gaze away, turning a
confused look to his brother.

Gerrald was grinning from ear to ear. "I never said what you
were looking at. I just said you were glaring. You, however,
make it sound like you were glaring at someone in particular.
Who would it be, I wonder..." He said, tapping his chin
thoughtfully with his goblet.

Arulean glared and then looked away, eyes finding the group
again. "You know very well who I am glaring at."

"So you admit you're glaring."

Arulean bit his tongue, grinding his teeth. "You seem
adamant about pointing it out, so I see no reason to deny it."

"Has he done something wrong?"

"No..."

"Then why are you glaring at him like he just put poison in
your drink?"

"I'm not glaring at him."

"You just said-- ah, I see."

"See what, pray tell?"

"You're glaring at those around him." Gerrald said.

It wasn't a question, so Arulean didn't bother answering. It
had been two days since their first kiss, entangled in the
gardens, alone, and distanced from everything. It felt like a

dream. Had it not been for the sly glances and playful, knowing quirk of his lips whenever Rajiah caught his eye, he would think it had been a dream. It felt too surreal to be true. The bubbling of happy warmth in his chest, the fluttering of butterflies, the nauseating nervousness, the buzzing of contentment and excitement in his veins... they were all feelings that he hadn't felt in a long, long time. Things he never thought he would feel again. Things he thought he was numb to until Rajiah Bronze flew into his life.

It was a simple social gathering after the usual nightly feast. It was nothing too formal, and, as such, Lyphnia hadn't seen any reason to stay glued to his side. She also seemed to have calmed down after the incident where he had blatantly chosen Rajiah's side over hers on the issue of the werewolf pack. She no longer hovered at his side and glared at her younger brother, but she did give them both a noticeable distance. Even now, she wasn't at Rajiah's side, attempting to pawn him off on alphas as she had been. She left him to his own devices, instead busying herself with hushed conversation with older, influential dragons.

Arulean was wary of that. He knew she was plotting against him, no doubt in an attempt to get more to her side to back her opinions and ideas during the official meetings. Under normal circumstances, he might try to counter balance her, perhaps go and interrupt her to keep an eye on things. This, however, wasn't under normal circumstances. Not when a sickening jealousy was burning like an itch beneath his skin at every admiring look an alpha sent Rajiah's way, not with the anger that bubbled in his gut when one of them reached out to casually touch him, not with the way everything in him was screaming to take the omega away and claim him.

He held himself in check though, firmly rooted to the spot,

simply watching and glaring from afar. He would deal with Lyphnia later, for now, Rajiah's entourage had his full attention.

He was remaining calm for the moment, but he wasn't sure what he would do if one of them attempted to leave with Rajiah alone.

Logically, he knew that Rajiah wouldn't want to do that anyway. He knew how the omega felt about his admirers. Logically, he knew that he had no right to him. No right to stop other alphas from courting him, no right to claim him. He could. No one would fault him for taking on another mate. Not with the obvious distance between him and Lyphnia. But he also didn't want to open up that opportunity for her to get out from under his influence.

So he watched from afar and brooded like a man half his age.

"Perhaps you should go talk to him..." Gerrald suggested, pulling him out of his thoughts.

Arulean scoffed. "That wouldn't look obvious at all."

Gerrald's eyebrows shot up, lips curling into an amused smirk. "Sarcasm? This must truly be serious. You, my dear brother, are smitten."

"I am not." The lie was weak.

"You are. I can see it in the way you look at him. Your body and your aura give it all away." Arulean glanced at him sharply, but Gerrald put up his hands defensively. "It's obvious to me because I've known you for so long. I doubt others can see it. But..." His smile widened. "I can also see the same smitten look when he looks at you."

I want you, Arulean Black. Arulean shivered, the echoes of that low, husky voice playing in his mind.

"You should steal him away." Gerrald said casually.

Arulean choked, coughing violently as he turned to gape at his brother. "I should what?" He sputtered, incredulous.

Gerrald eyed him sidelong before looking back across the crowd. He gestured to it vaguely with his cup. "You should steal him away."

Arulean frowned. "The risk of people noticing is far too high."

He shrugged, a smirk playing across his lips. "If you don't, we run the risk of you raging out on whatever poor, unsuspecting alpha decides to be bold and touch Rajiah." Arulean glared at him, lips pursed, but said nothing. He knew, deep in his heart, that his brother was right. Gerrald sipped his wine, eyeing Arulean over the lip of it with eyes that sparkled with mischief. "Besides, no one will notice if I distract them."

He blinked. "You would do that?"

Gerrald lowered his cup, his grin bright and cheerful. He clasped his free hand on Arulean's shoulder. "Arulean, my wise, yet naive brother, I've been trying to get you to chase your happiness for years. Now that we've found something that might just pull you back from the dark abyss of your own mind, you bet your damn throne that I would do anything to get you two together."

Arulean couldn't help the quirk of his lips. His shoulders relaxed. "Thank you, but..." He gazed out over the crowd, eyes flickering in his search for Lyphnia. She was nowhere in sight, something that should have worried him but he only felt relief. "I'm not too sure..."

Gerrald patted his shoulder roughly, laughing. "Nonsense! It'll be just like old times. Come on, Arulean, live a little."

"I am not--"

"I'm going," Gerrald said, already stepping away from him.

"Gerrald," Arulean hissed, reaching for him, but his brother danced away from his grasp, laughing.

He turned to look at him, eyes and grin practically oozing mischief. "Better make your move, brother." He said with a wink before turning on his heel and slipping into the crowd with a strange amount of fluidity and grace for a man his size. Arulean watched, internal war struggling as Gerrald got closer and closer to the group of people around Rajiah.

"Damn him..." Arulean cursed under his breath, knowing his mind had already been made up long before this moment. He slipped away from where he had been standing, weaving through the crowd toward the edges of the hall. He kept an eye on Rajiah, noting the moment that Gerrald exploded from the crowd with a wide grin and a boisterous greeting. He threw an arm over the shoulders of one of the alphas, pulling him close as he spoke to everyone in that odd friendly way of his.

As Arulean watched, Rajiah blinked at him, smiling at Gerrald but brows furrowing in confusion. Gerrald tilted his head as he spoke, and only Rajiah took the hint. His gaze swept idly across the crowd, lips pursed and brows furrowed, until his eyes locked on Arulean's. His lips relaxed, mouth forming a small, surprised o. Arulean smirked, making pointed eye contact, raising his brows, and nodding his head toward the exit. He held his gaze as he slowly turned, then broke away and slipped from the great hall. He hoped that was enough to get the message across.

Few people greeted him as he slipped away. He'd found that if he looked serious enough, and looked like he had places to be, people were less likely to approach him. This proved true once again as he made his way out to the inner hall. He found a place, close enough to the great hall that there were a few drifting dragons, but was otherwise empty. It was a hall, he knew, that was a favored spot for lovers. The hall was lined with alcoves, big enough for a couple to fit comfortably, and each alcove was sectioned off with a thick curtain that reached the floor. It was a design that had been for aesthetics, but the practicality of it was for visitors and partiers to have a place to escape and be alone. Arulean had never indulged in the hall himself. He saw it more of something for young couples and new couples, and this castle had been built at the height of his and Lyphnia's union. He'd never had a reason to venture here. Until now.

He made as if he was simply passing through, and when he was certain no one was in the open area of the hall, he slipped into an alcove close to the far end, one that he had determined was empty. And there he waited, leaning against the stone wall, feeling his heart hammering in his chest. He knew, logically, he had no reason to feel nervous. And yet he was. It was a strangely foreign yet oddly familiar feeling.

He knew when Rajiah got close. He could smell him through the crack he had left between the curtain and the wall, could hear his hesitant and light, careful steps, could feel his strong and warm aura. He peeked through the crack, knowing that the shadows of the alcove would hide him from view in the hallway. When Rajiah stepped in front of his hiding spot, his hand shot out, grabbing his wrist firmly and giving him a strong pull into the alcove. In a fluid motion, he pulled the curtain closed and pushed Rajiah up against the wall with his body, shoving a knee between his thighs and slapping a hand firmly over his mouth to cut off the shout of protest that came shortly after.

Rajiah struggled for a moment, body squirming fiercely, nails digging into the fabric and flesh of his arms. His eyes blazed in the darkness, aura flaring. And, all at once, everything seemed to click. Arulean wasn't sure if he noticed his scent or if his eyes adjusted to the darkness, but either way, Rajiah's squirming suddenly stopped, body relaxing and slumping against the wall, eyes widening, grip on his arms relaxing.

Arulean quirked a small smile in the shadows. "I am going to move my hand." He breathed, voice strangely muted in the secret space within the wall. The curtains were designed to hide scents and block sounds, to keep the secrets they held. "Try not to scream, will you?"

He moved his hand slowly, revealing Rajiah's pursed lips. "What are you doing?" He hissed, disgruntled.

Arulean smirked, leaning back a fraction to gesture vaguely to the alcove. "Rescuing you. I thought that much was obvious."

Rajiah glanced around, eyes growing accustomed easily to the darkness as their kind was prone to do. He looked back to Arulean, one eyebrow raised and a small smirk on his lips. "Rescuing me? From what?"

"From the herd of alphas that never seem to leave you alone."

He tilted his head back a little, resting it against the wall. They were still so close. Arulean's body pressed up against him, reveling in the feeling of him, warm and inviting. "Were you jealous, Arulean?" He practically purred.

Arulean suppressed a shiver and scoffed. "Hardly."

"Mhmm..." Rajiah hummed, lifting a hand to trail his fingers along the edge of Arulean's face, tucking a stray strand of hair behind his ear. He tilted his chin up, and Arulean automatically leaned his head down. He could feel his breath on his lips. "And now that we're here... what're you going to do with me?"

"I was thinking about kissing you." Arulean said, voice low and husky, eyes focusing in on those deliciously plump lips. In the small enclosure, Rajiah's scent was nearly overwhelming, filling his senses and driving him insane, pulling him closer.

Rajiah's hands slid up his arms, locking around his neck. His back arched, pushing his body flush against Arulean's. "Then do it..." He said, breathless.

Arulean brushed their lips together, and Rajiah's automatically parted. He felt the omega shudder, heard his breath hitch, and felt something akin to fire burn through his veins. "This is dangerous," He whispered, lips moving against Rajiah's. "Risky..." His tongue snaked out, running along the omega's bottom lip and drawing out a breathy gasp. "We could be discovered."

"I don't care," Rajiah breathed, sounding completely wrecked, despite them having barely touched. Something about that made pride swell in Arulean's chest. "Do you?"

"No," Arulean growled, and he found that he truly didn't. Something about the danger made it all the more exciting. Besides, he already knew he wouldn't be able to resist, not with Rajiah so close, in his arms, clinging to him and already shuddering in anticipation. He would never be able to walk away now. He would be a fool to.

He kissed him then, long and languid and sweet, cupping the

back of his neck and curling his fingers into his hair to tilt his head to deepen the kiss. Just like he had the first time, Rajiah opened up to him easily, body becoming pliant and willing beneath his touch. He leaned into him, body arching and small, breathing sounds coming from his throat.

He took his time exploring the omega, making himself familiar with him all over again, finding out what licks and nips drew out the best sounds, what touches he liked best. He pressed his thigh between Rajiah's legs, and the younger man rutted against him eagerly, hips rocking as his breath came quicker. He bit at Arulean's bottom lip, and the alpha groaned, fingers tightening in his hair, yanking his head back to expose the beautiful curve of his neck.

He nibbled and licked and kissed his way along Rajiah's jaw, down the column of his throat, biting at his collarbone, nosing at the scent glands, smelling deliciously sweet and swelling beneath his skin. He found himself growling and growing frustrated at the multitude of bands and chains the omega wore. They were hiding so much of his scent, but at least at this distance, he was able to smell him properly. Rajiah squirmed between him and the wall, whines and needy sounds escaping his swollen lips.

Beautiful. He was beautiful. Beautiful and needy and desperate for him and him alone. He was never like this around the other alphas. He was standoffish and firm, stubborn and defiant. But just a few touches and Arulean could reduce him to this. He did this. He made Rajiah like this. And that thought sent a fire between his legs, cock already hard and aching as he pushed it against Rajiah, eager for friction.

How long had it been since he had felt like this? Desperate for release and rutting against someone like a prepubescent youth? Too long. Far, far too long.

Without really thinking, he sunk his teeth into Rajiah's neck, jaw clenching hard. Rajiah cried out, shoving his knuckles in his mouth to muffle the sound. He clenched his eyes closed, body arching into Arulean, free hand digging nails into his shoulder. He bit down harder, growling low in his throat, hands holding the man's body to him. He didn't let go until he tasted salty, copper tang of the omega's blood.

Rajiah gasped sharply, the air being let out in a low groan as Arulean released him, lapping and sucking at the spot until it made a sizable bruise. He then leaned back, admiring his handiwork, his mark. He had marked Rajiah. It was a temporary mark. It would fade with time and didn't hold the same sort of significance as a true mateship bond, but it was still a mark, and it still send something primal and proud spiraling through him.

He wanted Rajiah to wear the mark proudly, openly, scare off all the other alphas. He wanted his scent on him, mixing with his like it was here in the confines of the alcove. He wanted Rajiah to be his and his alone.

"You have nothing to be jealous of," Rajiah's voice was soft, amused, and breathy. Arulean's eyes jerked to his, startled out of his thoughts. Thoughts that must have been clear on his face for Rajiah to have been able to read him so well. His lips were curled into a small smile. His fingers played with the long strands of Arulean's hair. He leaned close, lips brushing against his. "I told you that you're the one I want."

He kissed down Arulean's jaw, and he tilted his head back automatically to give him access. Rajiah layered kisses down his throat, his collarbone, tugging aside his tunic to get to his chest. He scraped his teeth along the sensitive flesh, and Arulean shivered. He wanted Rajiah to bite down, wanted to be marked the same way he had marked him, but Rajiah didn't. And that was probably for the best. It would be much harder for Arulean to hide a mark like that from Lyphnia.

Rajiah's hands slid down his chest, tugging his tunic free from his pants and slipping his hands up and under. His fingers spread wide, reverently touching, mapping, exploring his stomach and chest. Arulean let him, head tilted back and lips parted as he panted, letting the omega in, letting him have him in such a vulnerable state, feeling the eagerness and desperate need radiating from Rajiah's every touch. He knew he had Arulean in the palm of his hand, and he wanted more.

Then suddenly Rajiah was pushing him away, and Arulean stumbled back, protest cutting off as his back was shoved against the stone wall, Rajiah immediately crowding him. And then the omega was dropping to his knees, hands eagerly unbuttoning and pulling down the front of his pants. Arulean gasped in surprise as his cock, hard and flushed, sprung free, immediately hit by the cool air before he felt the warm breathy pants of Rajiah's breath.

Before he could truly register what was happening, Rajiah's mouth was around him and swallowing him down.

Arulean's head whipped back so fast that it cracked against the cold stones, and he saw stars. He gasped, at a loss for breath but unable to regain it. One hand gripped the stones behind him, fingers like claws against the mortar, the other buried itself in Rajiah's hair, pulling tight. The omega groaned around him, sending vibrations through him that ripped a moan from his throat. His mouth was hot and tight, and his pace was vigorous.

He made the mistake of glancing down. He made eye contact with the man, gazing up at him through half-lidded eyes. His lips were plump and swollen and stretched around the thickness of his cock, and he watched himself slide in and out of him as Rajiah bobbed eagerly on his length. His hands splayed out on Arulean's hips to steady himself. When he had Arulean's attention, he locked their gazes and swallowed him all the way down, nose bumping against his body and burying in the hair there. Arulean felt himself push against the back of and down his throat, and, amazingly, the man didn't gag. Instead, he swallowed, throat muscles contracting around him, and Arulean had to close his eyes to keep from coming on the spot.

His hips jerked, and Rajiah groaned again, fingers light and encouraging on his hips. Arulean's fingers tightened in his hair, hips jerking at a pace that was brutal but gentle enough to avoid hurting him as he made love to the omegas mouth.

Arulean had always been a patient man, steady and stern, but here, under the influence of Rajiah Bronze, he could feel himself unraveling.

He came with little warning, stars bursting behind his vision and with a loud groan that he couldn't contain. Rajiah swallowed him down, and when he pulled off of his length, Arulean watched through dazed eyes as he licked up the rest from his fingers and chin, maintaining eye contact the whole time.

Arulean felt himself stirring again, cock twitching with interest. He had no doubt he could go again, but for now, he had an omega that needed attention.

He pulled Rajiah to his feet, pushing him against the wall and grabbing his thighs, lifting him until the omega took the hint and wrapped his legs around his waist. Then he devoured the man's mouth, tasting himself and smelling the omega's strong sweet scent as his hand practically ripped his pants in an attempt to free his cock. His fingers wrapped around it, hard and thick and leaking, and pumped his length at a pace that was brutal, until Rajiah was squirming and whining and swallowing all those sounds with kisses that bruised, pumped him until he was crying out Arulean's name in a choked gasp and spilling over his hand, and then kissed him through his orgasm. He kissed him until they were both breathless, and then he kissed him more, because he couldn't get enough of him, and he wasn't sure he'd ever get tired of the taste.

Lyphnia found him in his study the next morning. He had bathed thoroughly and gone for a flight to dry to make absolutely sure that Rajiah's scent no longer clung to his skin. Still, when she burst through his doors with her usual flourish, he found himself stiffening for a moment before he forced himself to relax.

"Lyphnia," He greeted, barely glancing up at her and instantly putting his hands down to stop the flourish of papers on his desk.

"Arulean," She said, voice neutral in tone but uplifted. It was the voice she used when nothing in particular was upsetting her. Which was good, he thought. She walked around his desk, sitting on the edge of it and crossing her long legs at the knee. She was close, but there was still oceans of distance between them. Once upon a time, this position might have been intimate, teasing. He would have grabbed her by the hips and pulled her closer. He did no such thing now. That time was long past. She looked over the papers on his desk, picking a few up and shuffling through them, her dark red eyes sharp. "What are you up to this morning?"

He gave her a look of small annoyance before turning back to the rolled scrolls and folded letters open before him. "I am looking over the information our people have brought us in regard to their movements and the movements of other paranormals throughout the world." He said, shifting through a few.

"Anything of interest?" She asked, actually sounding curious.

"You have already heard much of the complaints and news of our people through the audiences we've held."

She groaned lightly, rolling her eyes. "Yes, every little thing from who got a splinter to who broke a claw."

"There is other, bigger news."

"Some dragons have decided to group for safety, some have taken to living closer to human civilization to blend in." Her lip curled at that. He smirked and said dryly, "Yes, I didn't think you would be fond of that one. He pulled out a map he had been working on, a map of the known globe with marks on various countries and continents. "Based on the news we have gathered, I have been marking which locations seem to be safe and which ones are dangerous to settle. I have also marked where known paranormal seem to be so that can be taken into consideration."

"Smart," Lyphnia hummed, nodding as she looked over the map. "Anything else?"

And so he told her. It was mostly out of obligation. She may be only his mate in name, as they hadn't been lovers in centuries, but she was still a dragon queen. They might differ on many vital points, but she still had influence among their kind. So he told her of the things they had received word of. He told her of the movements of lesser shifters, the movements and ploys and wars of the vampires, of the plights of the witches and of the druids. He expected her to grow bored and excuse herself, but she sat and listened, eyes sharp and lips pursed in thought. He saw glimpses of the woman she truly was, because beneath all the hatred and flair and appearances, she was extremely smart and amazingly cunning. She had gotten as far as she had in life because of her charm and ability to navigate people and situations.

She was smart, and that's what made her dangerous.

For the rest of the morning, they spoke of all matters of paranormal existence and that of the ever-spreading humans. They carefully steered away from topics they knew would lead to arguments and conversations they had made a thousand times, and for once they actually had a pleasant and mature conversation. He didn't feel the same thrill of her presence as he used to, but he did find an odd comfort in simply having known her for so long.

"Have you seen Rajiah since the feast last night?" She asked conversationally after a silence fell among them.

Arulean glanced up from where he was organizing the letters they had just gone through into neat piles. She was idly gazing at the map he had made, a quill twirling in her fingers after having made a few additional marks herself.

"I have not," He said steadily. "Is he missing?"

She tapped the feathered end against her chin. "I don't think so. He simply wasn't in his rooms this morning when I went to see him."

Arulean breathed an internal sigh of relief at Rajiah's forethought. If Lyphnia had seen him with Arulean's mark still fresh on his shoulder, she would have asked questions. Even if she didn't suspect Arulean, she would suspect someone, and she would no doubt pester him until she got answers.

"Perhaps he spent the night with an alpha." She said, voice too casual and neutral to be natural. He didn't need to look at her to know she was watching him out of the corner of her eyes, gauging his reaction. She would have to be blind to not see the way Arulean was drawn to Rajiah, and he knew he was being tested. She was poking him, trying to rile him up, see his reaction to the association of Rajiah with another man. Luckily, Arulean knew the only person Rajiah had been with was him, and he wouldn't rise to the bait.

"Perhaps," He said, pulling of casualty much more efficiently. "They have been swarming him for weeks now. It would not surprise me if he finally chose one." He had chosen none of them. He had chosen him.

Lyphnia hummed thoughtfully, lifting her chin a fraction as she regarded him. "Indeed... I only hope he chose someone worthy of his lineage, someone who would be a good match. He's been known to be foolish and headstrong, stepping out of line and reaching for things that aren't his to take."

"He's not taking anything if it is willingly given."

Silence fell in the room, neither of them willing to break it but both of them feeling the tension. Then Lyphnia set down the quill. "The First Meeting is coming up soon." She said evenly.

"It is."

"Many decisions will need to be made in the wake of my mother's death."

"Indeed."

"Without the Elders around, and as the last dragon king and queen appointed by the late Elders, our word will hold much weight."

"It will."

"No doubt our decisions will be the decisions the others agree to."

"No doubt."

"Which means our kind would be stronger if we appeared under a united front. If we both stood together, as a strong pair, we could easily rule our kind, and no one would question us. We could shape the future of dragon-kind with our own hands, our word as law, just as we always dreamed."

"We could..."

There was a long pause, and then softer but resigned, "We won't appear as a united front on the matters of the future, will we?"

He sighed, turning to face her. "I am afraid not."

They gazed at each other, eyes locked, depths of their irises swimming with melancholy, at the loss of what once was and what will never be again. There was an understanding there. It was an understanding that they had spoken of many times over the past few centuries, and that neither of their opinions would change. And if neither would budge, then they couldn't unite. Not even for The Summit. They would enter the First Meeting as opponents on a political stage. Rivals, despite their bond.

"Then I suppose we will have to let the council decide."

He nodded. "I suppose so."

She left then, with silent steps and swirling skirts. The door closing behind her was a muted boom that he felt down to his bones. He could only hope that their bond would be enough for him to rein her in from making irrevocable mistakes.

CHAPTER
NINE

"Arulean?" Rajiah's voice echoed through the tunnels, coming back to him with muted and augmented tones. He glanced around warily, but he didn't see anyone. It was... strange. He was certain there should at least be acolytes around. But the tunnels were empty. "Hello?" Nothing but echoes came back to him.

The tunnels that led to the main burial chamber were like a maze. There were no signs to point his way, and he was pretty sure he got turned around more than once. For the most part, he followed the vague and cold trail of Arulean's scent and felt for the gentle pull of his aura deep within the mountain. His steps were hesitant and silent. He hated the sound of the echoing in the empty space.

"Arulean?" He repeated as he paused at the entrance to the burial chamber, one hand placed on the wall of the tunnel archway. He tried to keep his voice soft to avoid the echo, but it still carried. Arulean stood at the center, before the giant lodestone. He held his hands out, but Rajiah was pretty sure he wasn't touching it.

Rajiah took a step into the burial chamber, hesitating again as the familiar eerie feeling of the place surrounded him, sinking into his skin, scraping against his nerves. The hair on the back of his neck stood on end, hackles rising. There was so much energy in here, so much that he didn't understand. It was unconfined, wild, unfocused. It clung to him like a second skin, thick and suffocating. He couldn't shake it, no matter how much he pulled into himself.

"What are you doing here?" Came the answer, his voice deep and rumbling, cutting through the air with little echo. He sounded flat, blank, but not unnaturally so. It was less like his usually reserved nature, and more like he was in a trance, something deep and peaceful.

Rajiah envied him for being so at ease in here.

"I came to find you." He said, glancing around as he took a few more steps forward. He didn't see the keeper or his acolytes, nor could he feel their presences. It was only the two of them.

"How did you find me?" He asked, not mad, merely curious. He still didn't turn around or move.

"I saw you fly this way after the First Meeting."

"You were watching for me?"

"I was..." He didn't see the point in denying it. The Summit Meetings were held in the council room deep within the castle. The walls and doors were thick to keep conversations private, and once a Meeting began, the doors didn't open again until it was concluded. It was an all-day event with only a short break for servants to bring them food. Rajiah had been waiting on the roof, hidden from most eyes and avoiding everyone. He had a clear view of Arulean when the man took off from the castle after the Meeting. Several of the others also took to the skies to blow off steam, but Arulean was the only one who headed to the distant mountain that housed the burial chamber.

"And you followed me." It wasn't a question, but he didn't sound mad, so Rajiah pushed forward.

"Yes. You looked... upset." He hedged, inching closer.

"Upset is a strong word. I am merely... unsettled."

"Did the First Meeting not go well?"

"It went about as well as can be expected. It only brought to light things that I had already known, and it's been made clear that the path ahead of me will not be an easy one."

He sounded sad, voice laced with resignation and melancholy. Arulean said nothing more on the matter, and Rajiah got the distinct impression that he didn't want to talk about it. So despite the fact that Rajiah was burning with questions about the First Meeting, he accepted that now was not the time. So he changed the subject.

"Why did you come here of all places?" He tried to sound casual, but he knew he sounded as uneasy as he felt.

"I come here to think." He said, tilting his head back, dark hair falling over his shoulders as he gazed up at the cavern's walls. "This is one of the only places I am guaranteed to be alone."

"Oh..." Rajiah hated how small his voice sounded. He took a step backwards. "Perhaps I should leave..." He could feel the energy pressing on him from all sides, the atmosphere of the burial chamber heavy on his limbs, pushing against his chest.

"No," His voice wasn't a demand, nor was it a command. It was, oddly enough, something akin to a plea. Rajiah felt his feet rooted to the spot, and he knew he wouldn't be leaving. "Stay... please."

"Okay," Rajiah breathed. He glanced around, unable to shake the feeling of being watched, but seeing nothing and no one. "Doesn't this place... feel creepy to you?" He asked, honestly curious how Arulean wasn't affected.

The man chuckled, a deep rumble in his chest that broke through the melancholy atmosphere. "Not at all." He took half a step back, turning to face him. He held out a hand, beckoning him forward with a simple gesture. "Come, I'll show you."

Rajiah stepped forward without hesitation, reaching for his hand and feeling electricity shoot through him, flooding him with a buzzing warmth when his long, slender fingers closed around his own. He tugged Rajiah forward gently, pulling him up alongside him, positioning him in front of the lodestone. He then stepped behind him, standing so his chest was brushing right up against Rajiah's back. He loomed over him, which might have once been intimidating, but right now Rajiah felt nothing but safe and secure.

Arulean's fingers gently encircled his wrists, positioning his hands out toward the lodestone, palms facing it and fingers splayed wide. Then he shifted his hands so his palms were up against the back of Rajiah's, fingers lacing with his own. He shifted, lowering his head so that it hovered over Rajiah's shoulder, lips close to his ear so he could feel the man's breath.

"Here, in this chamber, lie the remains of many of our kind, from the time the valley was founded until today. Many Elders are buried here, many youths, many men, women, and children, many who fell to the wars and the purge." His voice was soft. It's soothing, but it also sends shivers down his spine. "This mountain was chosen because of the properties in the rock within the walls. It holds and resonates energies. Every dragon's ashes are buried in small holes in the walls, their energies seeping into the stone, permeating the air, and weaving together. The lodestone acts as a conduit, a method of focusing the wild, loose energy when we need to use it."

"Like when you make the call for The Summit?"

He nodded, hair brushing against Rajiah's. "Exactly. I can use it on my own, but our call is more powerful when Lyphnia adds her power to mine, helping to focus and amplify the energies of the chamber."

"So she can use the lodestone, too?"

"Theoretically, yes, she can, but she doesn't. The chamber frightens her, though she will never admit it. She is too proud for that. But, she is easy to read. She finds the chamber off-putting."

"She's not the only one..." Rajiah grumbled, fingers shifting in the air as he tried to focus on the vague buzz of energy coming off the stone. It like static energy ready to spark if he got close enough.

Arulean chuckled. "The energies here are nothing to fear. They can be... a little overwhelming at first, but it is something I have grown used to. They are the energies of our ancestors, of our kin, of friends and of family. I know they would not hurt me, and that they are only the ghosts and shadows of the soul, reaching out for a kindred spirit to cling to. There is nothing they can do to harm you."

"Then why does Lyphnia fear them?"

"I believe... it is not the spirits of the dead that haunt her, but her own guilt. How much do you know of our history, Rajiah? Of the wars and the purge?"

"Not much," He admitted. "I was born shortly before the wars began, and my mother kept me sheltered from most of it."

"It was the product of humans rising against us, seeing us,

and all other shifters and paranormals, as unnatural beasts, despite the fact that we have been around just as long, if not longer, than they have. They grew in numbers, they learned how to fight us. At first it was easy to bat them away. We were stronger, faster, and saw ourselves as smarter. Our pride was our downfall." His voice was soft, laced with a deep seated melancholy and sounding far away. Rajiah wanted to turn in his arms, wrap him up in an embrace, kiss him until he smiled again, but he didn't. He stood still and listened. "They had more numbers, and they were persistent. They learned, they built, and they created. They developed ways of fighting us, using our lack of pack tendencies against us. We are powerful alone, but they could overpower us.

"The purge was a time of no mercy, of humans hunting paranormals, and the top of that list was dragons. We were the most well-known, the biggest, our pride and vanity making us old enemies and easy targets. We were too proud to hide, like many of the other paranormals, so we fought back. We lost many."

He breathed a deep, shuddering breath, ducking his head until it was rested against Rajiah's. Rajiah leaned back into him, silently offering support. Arulean's fingers tightened in-between his.

"I was young and rash. I encouraged the wars and the fighting. I fought back for my people. I led them into battles where some never made it back. Lyphnia and I stood side by side at the forefront of the battles. We were the faces of the purge, the leaders in the time of bloodshed. We were strong together, but not strong enough to save our people, and not strong enough to win."

He sounded tired, far too tired with far too many regrets. Rajiah leaned back further, pressing into his chest. He tilted his head to the side, nuzzling the side of Arulean's head. There was the briefest quirk of his lips, a small, fond smile that was overshadowed with sorrow.

"There came a time when I grew tired of the fighting. My turning point was the death of our youngest child. She was young and beautiful, not even old enough to present, only a century in years. We didn't allow them to fly on their own, not during the time of wars, but she was stubborn, much like our kind and much like her mother. She flew too far from the valley, and she was shot out of the air. I was the one who found her body and brought her ashes back to this very chamber. There," He said, lifting their joined hands to point at a spot on the far wall. "There is where she rests. Her energy is still young and wild, the fire that she never got a chance to grow into."

"After that, I wanted the fighting to end. It was clear we were not winning, and in the process, we were losing more and more of our kind. We have long lifespans, but we do not reproduce as quickly as we were losing lives. I realized what we were too blind to see before: we needed to hide. We no longer ran the world, and we couldn't afford to keep trying. We needed to move on with the times, and accept our place should we want to keep our kind alive. The other shifters and paranormals had already faded into the background, learning to adapt to live amongst and around humans without being seen. Humans are scared of what they do not understand, of what is different, and when they are scared, they act out in violence. We couldn't, we can't, afford to let them destroy us because of our petty pride.

"I tried to talk sense into Lyphnia and the others. I had about half of our kind on my side, the kind that was tired of fighting and tired of the bloodshed, the half that could see this fighting was leading nowhere except to our graves. The other half, unfortunately, stood behind Lyphnia. They were driven by rage, grief and bitterness twisting into a fuel for their fire. She called me weak, I called her blind, and we realized then that we were two very different people who would never be the same. We were no longer young and carefree, and as adults, we stood as opposing forces.

"She led her followers into a final assault, a final attempt to gain ground and regain land and power from the humans. It was a long, grueling assault. One that lasted years. She and the others were gone while the rest of us waited, feeling the loss of each of our kind deep in our hearts as their energies pattered out of existence. And we grieved and we waited."

"When she finally made it back, she had lost more than half of her company, and had only managed to recover most of their ashes. She came back defeated and tired, accepting that we had to retreat but not being happy about it. She's held a fire in her soul ever since then, and there are many others that feel the same. We haven't had official fighting since then, but there are incidents that happen, dragons who lose control, who lash out, who are discovered, and then they die, and their ashes are brought here. At every Summit, Lyphnia has tried to gather enough support to launch another assault, but we always arrive at a stalemate. She has never gained enough backing before, but I worry about our future. With the death of the last Elder, there is more fear and rage at our dwindling future than ever before."

He sighed, turning his head to nuzzle into Rajiah's hair, nosing his way through the thick, dark strands. He breathed his scent, sighing again as his body relaxed against his back.

"I have never forgiven her..." He said softly. "I have never forgiven her for drawing out the fighting, the wars... dragging our children into it. We lost so many, and with each of them, part of my heart died. When we stood apart, she coerced several of them to her side. They were enraged at the death of their youngest sister, and she fueled that rage into hate and into action. We lost all who sided with her, and she brought their ashes back to me in her shame, yet she has never apologized or regretted what she has done."

"I come to this chamber to find peace. I find comfort in being surrounded by the familiar energies of family and friends alike. It is the last place in which I can be close to them. In the sorrow of the past, I see what I have to protect, I see a reason to keep fighting for our future. I believe what Lyphnia sees when she comes here is the evidence of her failure. She feels guilt, and guilt keeps her from pursuing what she believes is the right course of action. And in there lies another of our biggest differences. I look to the past to guide me into the future, and she turns a blind eye to the past, no doubt sealing her fate in repeating it."

His aura was dark, his scent thick and heavy. It wasn't the vibrant, strong presence he had come to expect from Arulean. Here, he was vulnerable. Here, he allowed his follies to be on display. He opened himself up to Rajiah, and he wasn't going to take that lightly. His heart ached for the alpha, for the weight on his shoulders. He knew the history of their kind wasn't a pleasant one, but he truly believed their future would be alright if it was in Arulean's hands.

He couldn't erase the past, but he could comfort him now, in the present.

He turned in Arulean's arms, hands sliding up his arms, to wrap around his neck. He dug his fingers into the man's hair, gently tugging him down and kissing him, slow and languid, sweet and gentle. Arulean let out a shuddering breath against his lips before pushing forward. They came together again and again, light touches, almost chaste.

Then Arulean pulled away, just enough to put some distance between them. His head remained bowed, eyes shut. He breathed another shuddering sigh. "She and I are not lovers," He said softly, voice shaking slightly, as if he were admitting a truth that he had never dared to say aloud. "We have not been in centuries, but I cannot break our bond. Our bond is the only thing I have to keep her from running rampant. For the sake of our kind... I cannot..." He sounded like the words pained him to say.

"Come with me," Rajiah said softly, stepping away from him and taking one of his hands in his own. He continued to step away, Arulean stumbling after him, face contorted in uncertainty. Rajiah held eye contact until he was certain Arulean would follow, and then turned around, leading him out of the burial chamber, fingers intertwined. He led him out of the tunnels, following the smell of fresh air to guide him.

When they stepped out of the caves, night had fallen. Rajiah lifted his chin, breathing in the cool, night air, eyes drifting closed for several long moments. He let go of Arulean's hand and took several steps away from him before grabbing for the hem of his shirt. He pulled it over his head in one fluid motion and tossed it haphazardly to the ground. He kicked off his boots and shed his pants in much the same fashion.

Arulean said nothing, and neither did he move.

Rajiah reached the top of the stone carved steps that led down the mountain and began stripping off his jewelry, lying the pile with more care into one of his discarded boots. Then he stood and turned to face him. Arulean was still in the shadows of the mountain, light from a nearby torch flickering fire across his pale skin. He didn't bother to hide how his dark eyes roamed slowly up and down his body. Rajiah let him look, reveled in it, felt desired under the weight of those dark eyes.

"Fly with me." Rajiah breathed, knowing Arulean would hear him. It was an offer, and it wasn't just for a simple flight. And he knew that Arulean would know that.

The alpha's eyes drifted back to his face, searching his gaze. He said nothing, but his lips pursed, brows pinching just a fraction. His hands clenched and relaxed at his sides. Rajiah could see the internal debate flaring behind his impassive mask. Rajiah took several slow steps toward him, letting his body sway as he did so. He held out a hand.

"Fly with me," He repeated.

Arulean stared at him, from his outstretched hand to his face. Despite the war happening behind his eyes, Rajiah could smell the decision in his scent, smell the desire as his alpha pheromones flared. Rajiah could feel his own body reacting to it, heat shifting beneath his skin. The fire was only stoked brighter as Arulean's eyes swept over his body once again. He hated when alphas looked at him like that, but he loved it when Arulean did it. It makes him feel desired, powerful, beautiful. Heat surged downward, cock twitching with interest.

Arulean's eyes met his, hard and unwavering, burning with a fire that Rajiah could practically feel. "I cannot promise you anything..." He said softly.

"I'm not asking you to," Rajiah replied. His lips quirked into a small smirk, head tilting to the side to expose his neck, where the fading evidence of Arulean's mark was dark in the moonlight. "Fly with me."

He said nothing, but after only a moment's hesitation, he reached for the hem of his shirt, pulling it over his head. Rajiah took a moment to admire his chest, eyes shamelessly raking over the broad shoulders, well-muscled chest, toned stomach, and down to the narrow waist, lined on either side by the deep V of his hips. He could feel his body reacting to the sight, eager to simply rush him now, let him take him, but more than that, he wanted to tease, to draw it out, to make him chase.

So he lowered his arm, lips curving into a mischievous smirk as he met Arulean's eyes. Then he turned on his heel, ran the last couple feet to the top of the stairs, and launched himself into the air, shifting and twisting before throwing his wings wide to catch the breeze. He glided down the mountain for a moment before twisting, flapping, circling back up. He flew over Arulean, threw back his head and roared his challenge, and then darted away, cutting through the night sky like a knife.

It wasn't long before Arulean took to the air. He could feel him behind him, presence strong and wide wings disturbing the wind. He glanced back for only a moment, only long enough to truly admire him in all his glory, to feel the desire flame flare anew, before turning back around and giving his all to the chase.

He was small and quick, but Arulean was large and strong. He caught up easily on straight flights, but Rajiah would twist and turn, changing direction in sharp turns that Arulean couldn't imitate. He dove and rose with the wind, leading Arulean around, letting him get close enough to flick his face with his tail before changing direction. They darted across the night sky, two dark shapes obscuring the stars, moonlight glittering off their scales. They flew, weaving around each other, enjoying the wind under their wings and the weightless feeling of being alive. They were far from the valley. No one ventured out this way to the burial mountain. Here, they were free.

Rajiah wanted him. He knew, in the end, he would let Arulean catch him, but no matter how hot he burned, no matter how much his need ached, he kept flying, kept leading Arulean, a primal need to make his alpha fight for him, chase him, work to prove himself worthy driving him onward. Arulean trailed faithfully after his scent, growling when Rajiah slipped past him, growing more frustrated, more desperate. Rajiah could smell his own aching need in his scent. It drove him wild.

When he had reached his own limit, his body wet with need and hard with desire, he shifted his course and rose straight upward, wings flapping violently in his attempt to gain as much height as he could. Arulean rose after him, great wings pounding the wind in mighty beats. He rose, higher and higher, until the air was thin and the air chilled the moisture on his scales. He rose until his lungs burned and his wing muscles ached. He rose until he was somewhere between the ground and the heavens, and it was like a strange limbo between space and time.

And then he stopped, shot his wings out to let himself hover in the air.

He didn't have to wait for long. Arulean was right on his tail. He collided with him, wrapping his larger wings around him, and Rajiah curled his into his back. Their arms and legs intertwined, claws scrambling at scales. Their tails wrapped around each other, Arulean's longer length holding him captive. Rajiah automatically tilted his head back, and Arulean's jaw closed around the sensitive vulnerability of his neck. He clenched enough to be firm, to let Rajiah know he could kill him if he wished, and Rajiah didn't move, relaxing in his grip, letting himself be bare and vulnerable to him, to his chosen alpha.

And then they fell.

The fall was unlike anything Rajiah had ever experienced. The weightlessness, the lurch in his gut as gravity took hold, the feeling of helplessness as the alpha curled around him, plummeting with him. They fell fast, wind whistling through their ears, but they were so high up that he had no fear of hitting the ground. They were a tangle of scales, claws, and heat, intertwined and twisted, falling together in the space between the heavens and earth. Alone together, nothing existed but each other. And as Arulean's hard length unsheathed in his dragon form, adjusting so he could prod it against Rajiah's entrance.

He'd never done anything in his dragon form, nor had he done much in his human form, but instinct was a powerful thing. He arched his back, latching onto Arulean with claws and teeth, and relaxed, allowing the alpha to slide into his slick, wet heat. The feeling of being filled and stretched with Arulean's hard, thick length, combined with the low growl rumbling from his throat, made Rajiah dizzy. He held on, unable to much more, while they fell, connecting on levels he had never before experienced.

The ground came up fast, time was a blur, whizzing past and yet staying completely still. His ears rang with the wind, with the sound of the earth coming up fast. His mind told him to flare out his wings, to slow his descent, to curl up for impact, anything. But his instincts told him not to move, to trust his alpha. His mind screamed at him to do something, but his body was buzzing with dizzy pleasure.

Turns out, his instincts were right.

Arulean coiled around him. He was easily over twice the size of Rajiah, and when he wrapped him up, he was curled and protected. He flared out his own wings, slowing their combined descent much faster than Rajiah could do on his own. But he didn't slow them completely. If anything, he merely directed their fall so they would land in a clear space without trees. Right before they hit, Arulean rolled them so he was on the bottom, back to the earth and Rajiah curled protectively against his underside.

The impact was jarring. They hit hard, vibrations rattling them down to their bones as the earth gave way, denting and creating a crater. Dirt and dust was thrown up into the air, suspended for a moment before raining down on them. Rajiah barely noticed. Arulean was still inside him, and the impact buried him deep. He hissed and gasped, spine arching as he writhed on top of the alpha.

He wasn't sure what possessed him to do it, what signal went between them, who started it first, but a strange under-standing passed between them, a buzzing of energy, and they shifted together. The shift was strange. Arulean remained inside him.

When the shift completed, bones popping back into place, smoke drifting from their skin and disappearing into the night air, he was perched on top of the alpha, his thick member buried deep in Rajiah's wet heat, stretched and filled but so good. He put his hands on Arulean's chest, back arching as he gasped, trying to catch his breath and steady his pounding heart. Arulean lay under him, eyes devouring him, half-lidded and heavy with hunger. His hands roamed up and down Rajiah's thighs with surprising gentleness, but with an edge reverent possession.

"You are so beautiful," He murmured, voice low and husky, crackling like static across Rajiah's skin.

He bent over then, hovering just over him, lips just a breath apart. "As are you." He kissed him then, hard and hungry, nipping at the alpha's lips and pushing his tongue into his mouth. Arulean growled, returning the kiss in kind, hands roaming over Rajiah's body, his back, nails biting, grip bruising, constantly moving like he couldn't quite get enough. Arulean's scent was thick and heavy in his nose, drowning him and making him dizzy. He ground his hips down as they kissed, nails digging into Arulean's chest as the alpha's hips jerked up against him.

When he felt like he couldn't breathe, he leaned back with a gasp, breaking their kiss as he sat up. He gazed down at Arulean, pale skin flushed, dark hair mussed, dark eyes glimmering with desire, bruised lips parted and wet, chest heaving as he panted. He looked like an absolute wreck.

He had done this. He had make Arulean like this. He had brought the powerful, stoic, dragon king Arulean to his knees with desire.

Something inside him stirred, that shifting and preening of pride, fueling his own hunger, making him want more. He wanted Arulean to lose all control of himself, for him to be completely at his mercy and no one else's.

I want him to be mine.

With small encouraging movements from Arulean's hands, Rajiah started to ride him. He started out slow, feeling the delicious drag of Arulean's cock as he lifted himself, and gasping at the thrust as he let himself drop. Arulean was thick and filled him completely, stretching him beyond what he thought he was capable of. But he was wet and eager, and he could deal with any soreness in the morning. So he lifted himself up again, holding it for a moment with just the head of his cock inside, and then let himself drop again, bottoming out as he threw back his head and gasped, back arching.

He set a rough pace, rising and falling and rising as fast as he could, until his thighs were shaking and his breath came in shallow pants. His nails dug into Arulean's chest in a desperate attempt to keep himself up. His body shook, head tossed back and eyes closed, but still he kept going, chasing the feeling of Arulean inside him, unable to stop, unwilling to give in. Arulean's hands were on his hips, claws digging into his sides as he lifted him up before pulling him back down, lifting his hips to meet Rajiah's.

Then suddenly he was moving as Arulean flipped them over, rolling on top of him and pressing Rajiah's back into the dirt.

Rajiah automatically wrapped his legs around Arulean's hips, arms wrapping around his neck and fingers burying in his hair as he tugged the man down for a sloppy, but hungry kiss. With one hand on his hip and the other holding him up, Arulean thrust into him. His pace was quick and merciless, hips snapping forward with quick precision. Rajiah arched into him, his kisses becoming quickly uncoordinated as he panted, gasps and moans ripping from him, choked off with small cries. Arulean devoured the sounds before nosing Rajiah's head aside, diving in toward his neck. His tongue and lips dragged along the sensitive skin there, and Rajiah shuttered when he pressed over his swollen scent glands. Then the alpha bit down, bruising and hard just as he thrust in deep, and Rajiah let out a strangled cry.

"Arulean--" Rajiah gasped out, voice shaking and hoarse, trembling as he struggled to form coherent words. "Arulean-- please-- I can't-- fuck—more---Arulean--"

The man growled, biting down harder before releasing him, licking along the mark and latching on with his lips to suck. Rajiah moaned, tilting his head to the side as his nails dug into Arulean's shoulders, scratching and clawing his back with everything he had. He tried to move with the man's thrusts, hips working together for just moments before Rajiah couldn't keep up and simply let Arulean take him without mercy.

A familiar heat was building low, coiling and threatening to push him over the edge. He was achingly hard, his cock bouncing against his stomach and leaking. His nails dug into Arulean's back, fingers of one hand twisting in his hair and tugging until the alpha growled against his neck. "Arulean-- fuck-- I'm gonna-- I'm close--"

He tilted his head, lips brushing his ear, teeth nipping at his lobe. "Come for me, Rajiah." His hand relaxed its bruising grip on his hip, drifting across his stomach to wrap long, slender fingers that were hot to the touch around his aching cock. His back arched just a little more as he gasped, breath lodging in his throat.

He was so warm. So, so warm. Warmth inside him, warmth around him, warmth on top of him. Heat and fire, building, building, building, threatening to combust and consume him. He tried to croak out Arulean's name, but it came out as mangled and incoherent syllables. He kept trying though, stringing together half formed words and pleas between gasps and strangled moans.

"Come for me," Arulean repeated, thrusts becoming uncoordinated and rough, hand slipping as he pumped him hard. "Come for me." He tilted his head, nuzzling his nose just under Rajiah's ear. He could feel him panting against his skin, feel the vibrations of his voice. He squeezed his eyes shut, entire body coiling and tensing.

"Arulean--"

"Rajiah--" His name was both a curse and a prayer as it fell from Arulean's lips, voice low and broken, a plea and a command.

He came suddenly, stars igniting behind his eyelids and body wracking in quakes as he rode out his orgasm, spilling over Arulean's hand and clenching tight around him. He bit down on Arulean's shoulder, teeth sinking into flesh as his jaw clenched tight. His throat felt raw. Raw enough that he knew he must have made a sound, but he couldn't hear it over the ringing in his ears. Fire sizzled over his skin, igniting a flame that burned through him.

Arulean's thrusts became erratic, less coordinated, until suddenly he thrust deep and came with a strangled cry that nearly sounded like Rajiah's name. Warmth spread through him as Arulean thrust shallowly and weakly through his orgasm. Rajiah coaxed him through it, rubbing up and down his arms, his back, his sides, running fingers through his hair as he whispered sweet nothings, words that he couldn't remember and barely understood himself.

And then Arulean collapsed on top of him, chest heaving as he struggled to catch his breath. His face remained buried in Rajiah's neck, nose against his throat and breath caressing his collarbones. He was heavy and large, making breathing difficult, but Rajiah didn't mind. He basked in the afterglow, hands and fingertips caressing Arulean's skin, feeling the softness of it, of the hard muscles beneath, weaving through his hair and scratching at his scalp.

When Arulean slipped out of him, Rajiah was unable to stop

the whine that escaped his throat. He wanted Arulean to stay in him for longer, wanted to feel filled, wanted his knot to lock them together for the entirety of the night and into the early hours of the morning, wanted to be filled again and again and drive him crazy and wild.

But he knew he couldn't. Arulean had already attacked his scent glands, melding their scents and claiming him there, marking him. If he were to take the alpha's knot... by dragon standards, they would be mated. And if they mated, Arulean's hold over Lyphnia wouldn't be as complete. Rajiah understood this, understood why it couldn't happen, but it didn't stop him from feeling empty and incomplete over the loss of Arulean inside him.

But then the alpha was lifting himself up onto his elbows, gazing down at him with eyes that saw nothing but him, black pools that glittered and shone, eased at the edges with fondness and contentment, lips relaxed and curved just slightly, like he wasn't even aware he was doing it. And when he touched him, his caress was so gentle, so soft, like Rajiah was something precious that might shatter if he pressed too hard. He touched his chest, his shoulder, his neck, fingertips moving up his jaw to cup his cheek.

"You're beautiful," He breathed, voice hoarse and low, but cracking with honesty.

Rajiah put a hand over his, holding it there as he leaned into the touch. His free hand lifted, brushing hair away from the man's temple and trailing down to cup his cheek, thumb brushing over the high, sharp bone. "So are you," He said softly, lips curving into a gentle smile.

"We should get back..." He said, though reluctance and hesitance was thick in his voice.

Rajiah's legs tightened around him. "Not yet," He said, voice firm and commanding, and surprisingly, Arulean relaxed into him. He pulled the alpha down for a kiss, then whispered against his lips. "Tonight, is ours. Tonight, think of me and only me. Tonight, make me yours."

"I cannot make you mine..." Arulean said as though it pained him, voice cracking and shuddering with regret.

Rajiah only tugged him closer. "You already have."

He cut off Arulean's protest with a kiss, reveling in pride as the alpha melted against him.

They didn't make it back to the castle until the sun had already risen high over the valley, their bodies marked, bruised, and sore, but their hearts light and happy.

CHAPTER
TEN

Rajiah didn't see much of Arulean for the next couple of days. It wasn't, however, from lack of trying.

He tried to catch Arulean's eyes several times, tried to catch him in their usual places, and was disappointed to find the man avoiding him. He supposed he couldn't blame him too much. Lyphnia was watching them heavily. He could feel the weight of her suspicious gaze weighing on him wherever he went. After they had returned after their amazing night together, he had bathed and soaked thoroughly to remove most of Arulean's scent, and he was certain the other man had done the same. Still, the marks remained. The marks made from hands, nails, and teeth. He dressed more conservatively than normal to hide most of them, wrapping scarves around his neck beneath his gold bands.

He understood Arulean's hesitance. Rajiah had made things difficult for him by saying he was Arulean's. And whether it could have been brushed off as a heat of the moment declaration, it still rang true. And Rajiah had meant it. He knew he couldn't be Arulean's mate in truth, but he was the only man, the only alpha, who had ever made Rajiah feel this way. Made him feel anything at all. He didn't want to give that up. He wasn't sure he could.

He had always been a wanderer, exploring the world and meeting new people, but never finding a place of his own. He didn't find a home among dragons, and his homes with other shifter packs were always temporary. When it came down to it, he wasn't one of them. He never felt a place he belonged, despite loving the places he had been. Yet with Arulean... he felt like maybe he could have something he never had before. A spot inside him that he had never realized was empty suddenly felt full.

So he gave Arulean the space he needed. That, however, didn't stop him from being drawn to him, from being tugged toward him by invisible strings. Whenever he wasn't paying attention, he ended up near Arulean or one of their spots. Several times he dragged himself out to the valley to visit the packs and shifters he knew, but even then, his mind and eyes kept drifting back to the castle on the hill.

At evening feasts, Arulean didn't approach him, but he felt the alpha's eyes on him always, a burning presence on his back as his suitors tried to get his attention. He smiled and spoke on autopilot, keeping his attention on Arulean throughout it all. He stood a little straighter, smiled a little brighter, when he knew the man was watching. He wanted Arulean to want him, and he wanted Arulean to know that he wanted him.

Whenever their eyes met, Rajiah felt lightning flash through him, setting his insides ablaze and tingling out across his skin. If he ever doubted how Arulean felt about him, he only had to make eye contact to feel reassured. The world was in those eyes, worlds of emotions and desires that he kept on a tight leash, but which he couldn't quite hide from his eyes. He felt it in the lingering stares, in the way his face softened when their eyes met.

Rajiah couldn't, however, stay away forever.

The Second Meeting of The Summit was several days after the first. He waited around anxiously from dawn to dusk. Unable to stay still, he paced the castle, feet tapping lightly on familiar flagstones. He avoided others, using the action to amuse himself as he waited. Once the meeting was over, he watched from perch outside on a roof, watching as the dragons filtered out of the conference room and along the halls through the windows, watched them file out along the outer breezeways. There were many faces and many auras, but he found Arulean easily enough, trailing him as he went to his study. Once everyone was filtered out of the room and on their way, and after he made sure Lyphnia had gone elsewhere, he snuck back inside, ghosting along the hallways to Arulean's study.

As he approached, he heard voices, muffled by the thick doors and walls, but loud enough for him to pick out both Arulean and Gerrald's voices. Even with an ear pressed to the door, he couldn't make out the words, but they were shouted and hissed, snapping at each other with a rage that seemed to permeate the air. Unable to control himself and his curiosity, seized by a sudden burst of brash confidence, he pushed one of the doors open, stepping into the room.

Their conversation cut off abruptly, and Rajiah stood there, one hand on the door, as they looked him over. They both stood in front of his desk, faces flushed and postures bent and crooked in their anger. At the sight of him, they had two very different reactions. Arulean's expression pinched, closing off and becoming cold.

"What are you doing here?" He snapped, voice harsh in remnants of his argument. Even he winced at the sound of it.

Rajiah bristled. "I came to hear how the meeting went." He said bluntly, confident, like he had every right to demand this of the dragon king.

Gerrald's face, however, relaxed slightly. He sighed, resigned as he ran a hand through his hair. He glared at his brother, though it wasn't with fire so much as stubborn frustration. "I should go."

Arulean looked at him sharply. "There is no need--"

"I will speak with you later." He walked briskly away, stopping at Rajiah's side for a brief moment to put a hand on his shoulder and say in a low voice, "Perhaps you can talk some sense into him." And then he was gone, stepping quickly through the open door and shutting it behind him with more force than necessary.

"What happened?" Rajiah asked after a moment of silence.

Arulean wasn't looking at him. He leaned back against his desk, legs crossed at the ankles and arms crossed over his chest. He was looking at a spot across the room. "Nothing you need concern yourself with..."

Rajiah's brows furrowed as he glared, lips pursing into a frown. "Bullshit." Arulean blinked, looking at him with surprise. Rajiah crossed the room with long, purposeful strides, stopping when they were face to face. He jabbed a finger into Arulean's chest. "Whatever is happening in those meetings will affect all of dragon-kind. Including me. So it is my business." His face softened, and he tried to smile. "And whatever it is, it's obviously upset you. What happened?"

Arulean looked him over, expression blank as he searched Rajiah's face. Then he sighed, pinching the bridge of his nose between two fingers. "It is just... Lyphnia, as usual."

"What has my sister done this time?"

He scoffed in dry amusement. "Just the usual, only this time she is actually getting somewhere with it."

Rajiah frowned. "What does that mean?"

Arulean sighed again, letting his hand drop. He stared at the ceiling. "I proposed the Paranormal Pact."

He tilted his head to the side. "The what?"

"It is a pact that has been proposed and spread among the paranormal community. It is the idea that we keep ourselves hidden from humans, we blend in or avoid them and do not make our presence known. It is done with the hopes that, over time, they will forget we existed altogether. We will fade into myths for them, and they will live without the knowledge that they are living alongside creatures that are not human. This is done with the idea of preservation in mind. If they do not think we exist, then they will stop hunting us.

"Humans are very prevalent and resilient creatures. We are stronger, but they outnumber us. They are many, and they are strong in those numbers, and they only continue to spread. Things cannot be as they once were. I am trying to move our kind into the future, while Lyphnia attempts to reclaim the past."

"I take it she didn't like the idea of this pact?" Rajiah asked wryly.

"No, she finds it abhorrent, and any creature that abides by it to be weak. The vampires have just recently started to accept the pact, though there are covens that don't abide by it. The witches were the first to suggest it, and the witch hunts have lessened significantly. Humans scare easily. They scare and they lash out at what they fear. We must proceed with caution if we are to keep from dying out."

"Let me guess," Rajiah said, voice dripping with venom and simmering with rage. "Lyphnia turned the council against you and your idea?"

He shook his head. "Not quite. Not all of them. But more than half do not like the idea of the pact. They see it as weakness. Even if they do not want war as she does, and though they are hesitant to call to arms, they do not wish to hide either. We are dragons, and we are proud and vain. We like to be seen."

"Our pride will be our folly."

"I agree, but I am one man, and I cannot control them all."

"But why not?"

"Our kind does not work that way, Rajiah. We do not have one Alpha to rule the pack. We had Elders to watch over us and guide us. We had dragon kings and queens to give us direction and commands. But decisions such as this, large scale decisions, they are always determined by the council. I may have heavy influence, but so does Lyphnia. I cannot force them all under my control."

Rajiah's face scrunched up, lip curling in distaste. He didn't see why not. Arulean was clearly more powerful and influential than any of the others, including Lyphnia. She might be cunning and crafty, but Arulean commanded respect and wielded it like a second skin.

Arulean stared blankly at the ceiling, lines around his lips forming. "I will have to compromise." He said softly.

Rajiah gaped at him. "What?"

Arulean lowered his head to look at him. He looked resigned, defeated. "I have no choice. After I proposed the pact, there was already hesitance. Lyphnia was ready. She prayed on all of their fears and worries, stroking their pride and vanity. There was nothing I could do. By the end of it, she had more than half of the council behind her. I only had a fourth behind me, and the rest remained undecided. We have only one more meeting, and decisions will need to be made. She has been pushing for war again, a fight back to reclaim our territory, to shine brightly in the sun and let humans beware. She wants to teach them what it is to fear us again. She has been pushing for years, but the Elders always held her back after the wake of the purge. Without them, it is only me to hold her back, and I do not know if that will be enough. Too many of them are behind her."

"I will have to compromise. If our next meeting follows the same vein, we will go to war again. I have to think of a way to allow that, but also allow us some refuge and safety--"

"We can't go to war again!" Rajiah snapped, unable to contain it any longer.

Arulean's eyes focused on him, narrowing. "Do you think I do not know that?" He straightened a little, towering over Rajiah. "I have lost more to those wars than you will ever know."

Rajiah grit his teeth and didn't back down. He jabbed a finger into Arulean's chest, and the man blinked in surprise. "You promised you wouldn't let it happen again. You've dedicated yourself to keeping us from making the same mistakes, and after one fall back, you're willing to give in?"

Arulean pushed his hand away, lips pursing into an irritated frown. "I know when I'm beaten, Rajiah."

"But you aren't!" He shouted, running his hands through his hair and tugging at the strands. He spun on his heel, striding several steps away before turning, pointing at him accusingly. "You just said you know the pain of the wars more than anyone, and yet you're willing to let our people go into that again? And why? Because Lyphnia showed you up once in a meeting?"

"It has not just been once--"

"You're spineless, Arulean Black." Rajiah spat, eyes blazing and lips pressed into a firm frown.

Arulean bristled at that, eyes widening and jaw going slack in his shock. He blinked. "Excuse me?" He said, voice low and dangerous, full of warning that Rajiah blatantly ignored.

"I said," He said, seething with anger. "You are spineless. You talk big, you talk about sacrifice, you talk about keeping our kind safe, you talk about saving us from repeating the past, but when it comes down to it, you give up. You are spineless. All bark and no bite. What kind of dragon are you?"

He could see Arulean's anger. He could see it in the way he straightened, in the way his fists curled tight at his sides, in the way the lines tightened around his eyes as he glared, in the way his lips worked as he frowned, in the blaze of cold anger in his eyes. "You hold your tongue--"

"No!" He threw his hands up in the air. "I will not! You need to hear this and clearly, no one is willing to tell you."

Arulean stepped up to him, towering over him, pressing on him on all sides with his aura, enraged and flaring. Rajiah ignored him and stood his ground. Arulean's voice was ice. "You speak out of turn. I do not need to hear this from--"

"From who?" Rajiah snapped. "An omega? Well I'm the omega you have been pining after for weeks, Arulean. The omega who wants you but can't have you because you're so dedicated to keeping Lyphnia in check." He shoved Arulean, startling the man until he stumbled backwards against his desk. He stared openly at him, obviously surprised. Rajiah wasn't sure anyone had ever yelled at him like this, but he was too fired up to care. He pointed at him. "You want to keep her in check? Well it's time to check her. You talk big, like you have her on this leash. Now put that to the test and tighten that rope. You reject me so you can keep her, well what good is that if you won't press your advantage?"

"It is not so simple--"

"Bullshit. You say you can't force the entire council? Fine. You can't force your will on them all. But you can on her. That was the whole point of keeping your mateship bond alive. You are literally the only one who can stand against her. Force her to back down, and the others will lose their confidence. She is the spear point, so break that off. You're the only one who can."

"Rajiah--"

"No, you need to listen." He snapped, stepping up to Arulean, putting a hand on his chest to keep him sitting on the edge of his desk. It brought them closer in height, allowing for him to better meet his eyes. Arulean glared at him, anger simmering beneath the surface, but his expression was set in resignation. "She wants a war for revenge, to get back a life where she was more powerful. Those are the wrong reasons to put us in danger. You are right, Arulean. You have great ideas and everyone's interest at heart, but you are weak if you won't do anything about it.

"A war like this would affect so much more than our kin. A war would affect all shifters. As dragons, we are the most visible, but the others would catch the fall out. All shifters would be hunted, even those who want to fade into myth. Shifters like Marli and Regge. Shifters like that wolf pack we saved. They come here for protection. They come to you for protection. And yet you're willing to toss away that safety because you're too frightened to fight back with Lyphnia."

"I am not afraid--"

"You are! You're scared of failing again, Arulean. I know you are. And that's stopping you from trying. I know you're tired. I know you've been through so much, but you're not dead yet, and you still have the strength to go on, to protect us. Not just dragon kin, but all shifters. We all need you. All of us. It's not just about dragons anymore. It's about every shifter, great and small. And you're our only hope against a war that Lyphnia will create."

He stepped away, holding Arulean's gaze, fire burning in his eyes. He lowered his voice. "If we don't look after those weaker than us, then what good are we?"

Arulean said nothing, and Rajiah didn't give him a chance to. He turned on his heel and strode out of the room, letting the heavy oaken doors close behind him with a resounding bang that echoed throughout the hall. He realized he probably should have stayed, probably should have helped Arulean through this, listened to his thoughts, something, anything.

But he couldn't stay. There was an itch beneath his skin, a rage that simmered in his bones. He was mad at Lyphnia, he was mad at the council, and he was mad at Arulean. Arulean, who refused to mate with him because of his ties to Lyphnia, but who refused to use those ties to keep them from tumbling to their downfall. He hoped his words would have an impact because he couldn't stay still any longer, couldn't just sit around and talk. He was restless, his dragon inching toward the surface.

He went to his room, stripped off his clothes with little care, and stepped out to the balcony. He leapt into the air, letting the shift take him, and he flew out over the valley, pushing himself hard and fast, rising high until the air was thin and moisture crystalized on his scales, and then fell toward the earth, closing his eyes and letting the wind in his ears and against his scales erase his worries, if only for a few fleeting moments.

CHAPTER
ELEVEN

He found her in one of the lesser used hallways after the evening feast the next day. Rajiah, predictably, didn't show up, and that was like an itch beneath his skin, a reminder, making his words ring louder in his inner ear. His words had been haunting him all day, barely allowing him to sleep the previous night.

If we don't look after those weaker than us, then what good are we?

She was surrounded by several of her entourage. Some of them were members of the council, older and war worn, bitter and jaded men and women. Others were younger, not quite influential but eager to prove themselves. They were all followers. He could tell by the way they hung on her every word, recognizing some of them as her louder supporters from the Meetings. He approached them at an even pace, strides long, hands clasped behind his back, chin held high, lips pursed, and eyes like ice.

They all looked at him as he approached, silence settling over the group. Their expressions ranged from contempt, to curiosity, to fear, to indifference. Lyphnia was the only one who smiled, though it held no warmth. It was the sly smile of a victor, confident and cocky with no room for remorse or modesty. "Why, Arulean," She said as he stopped next to their group, making it clear that he wasn't simply passing by. "What a pleasure to see you." They both knew it wasn't.

"Lyphnia," He greeted, voice carefully blank. His eyes slid to the dragons around her. "May I have a word with my mate... alone?" He framed it as a question, but there was nothing but casual command in his voice. Most of them nodded, muttering honorifics and polite phrases as they dipped away. Several of them hesitated, glancing at Lyphnia and waiting for her to idly wave them away.

They locked eyes, neither one of them backing down or speaking until the others had cleared out of the hall.

"What are you doing, Lyphnia?" He asked when they were alone. He was unable to keep the sigh from his voice, feeling tired above all else. They had done this dance a million times. Had this conversation a million times.

She crossed her arms over her chest, leaning her weight to one hip as she tilted her head, gazing up at him. "I do not know what you mean, Arulean." She said innocently, still smiling, eyes sharp. Several of her deep red curls fell from their pins to frame her face. She was beautiful, like a deadly flower or a poisonous snake.

"I am tired of this dance, Lyphnia." He said bluntly, keeping his voice even. "You know very well what I mean. The Meetings. The war. Why must you push this foolish plan forward?"

"Foolish?" She said, smile dropping into a delicate frown. Her eyes hardened, and her posture straightened. "Is it so foolish to take back what is ours? To stop cowering? I do not know about you, Arulean, but I refuse to roll over with my belly up. We are dragons. We deserve our place in this world, and we deserve for it to be in the open. I do not wish to start a war, but I do not wish to hide."

"You know your actions will cause a war, whether you start it directly, you will start one nonetheless."

Her eyes sparked, crimson red glinting in the dark depths.

Her voice was cold and sharp, but heated with a simmering rage that had sustained her for years. "If a war is what the humans want, then so be it. We will show them that we are the superior race."

He sighed, shaking his head. "Have you no guilt, Lyphnia? No shame?"

She bristled at that, temper and aura flaring. "Have you no backbone, Arulean?" She spat.

His eyes narrowed. "Your ambitions and pride and greed are the reason why so many of our kind, of our children, are dead."

"Or," She said, voice low and seething. "Perhaps it is your cowardice, holding back so many of our forces and cutting our strength, that brought them to their graves."

He stiffened, breaths coming shallow as he struggled to keep hold on himself. He felt ice in his veins. "Do not blame this on me." He breathed, voice full of warning. Enough so that any other shifter, save perhaps Gerrald and Rajiah, would have backed down.

Her lips quirked in a wry, bitter smile. "You hold guilt in your heart because you are guilty. I did nothing wrong, and I will avenge those who wronged us, bringing forth a bright future for our kind. I believe the Second Meeting was proof enough that plenty will stand by me. This is moving forward, Arulean. With or without you." Her face softened then, shadow of sorrow somewhere in the depths of her eyes. It wasn't a plea, nor was it hope. It was a mourning of something that had long passed. "Though I wish you would reconsider. We could still be great together, Arulean. We could still have it all."

He held her gaze, feeling the weight of the past on his chest. He thought of Rajiah, of that bright young smile, of the happiness he felt when around him, of the hopeful outlook on a future without fighting, of how the omega made him feel alive again when he wasn't even aware he had felt dead. "You know that is no longer possible." He said softly, almost an apology.

She regarded him then, trying to mask her expressions, but he knew her too well. He saw the pain, the anger, the rejection swirling in her eyes. Then she steeled herself, lifting her chin. "I will see you around, then, Arulean." She said, brushing past him and heading down the hall.

He half turned to watch her go, feeling the weight of what they once had crumbling inside him. He hadn't realized he had been holding out hope, but now he recognized that he had. And now that hope was gone. She would not change, and he could not change her. She kept fighting for what she wanted, so he would to. He could not keep living like a ghost of the past. Not if he wanted to build a future for his kind and all shifters.

A future that he pictured with a certain dark haired, dark skinned omega at his side, with a smile that shone like the sun and eyes that blazed like fire.

"Will you ever change your mind?" He asked softly, unsure whether or not she would hear him.

She stopped, and turned her head to the side, not quite enough to look back at him but enough that he saw her profile. "No," She said softly, a small frown on her lips. "Will you?"

"No," He answered without hesitation.

She turned back around. "Then I will do whatever I can to do what I believe is right."

"As will I."

And with that, she left, and he let her go. Let her go from his heart, but not his life. He still needed to keep their bond alive. He needed it to keep her in check, and this time, he would use it. He would use it as Rajiah had said, because Rajiah was right. He was right about all of it. Arulean had lost his fire when Lyphnia drifted from him. But now, with Rajiah, he thought he might have found it again. He found a reason to keep fighting, to keep moving forward, to keep fighting for a future. For now, he would let Lyphnia relish in her self-proclaimed victory.

At the third and final Meeting, Arulean would bring that all crashing down.

Once upon a time, Arulean had been a man who had taken what he wanted. He had risen through the ranks of his kind, fighting his way to the top, becoming powerful and respected in the eyes of the Elders and his peers. He had fought for his position, he had fought for his kind, and then he had fought for peace. He had always seen what he wanted and allowed himself to take it. He was a dragon, after all. A dragon king, and a strong alpha. There were few things beyond his grasp. After the purge and Lyphnia's last stand, however, he had pulled in on himself, stopped allowing himself things that made him happy, contented himself to be idle and told himself that he was holding Lyphnia back by doing nothing.

Now it was time for him to take action against her, and he would.

For now, however, he would start with allowing himself to take the things he wanted, to take his own happiness. And that meant taking Rajiah.

The night air was cool on his scales as he circled the valley, high and gliding in wide sweeps. There were a few other dragons in the air, but they gave him a wide berth, and he flew above them all, as a king should. He let himself enjoy the night, to bask in the starlight and revel in the wind under his wings and the chill on his scales. He let his own anticipation build. Let it simmer and coil inside him, let it brew until he was practically quivering from adrenaline.

Then he tipped his wings and let the wind guide him down, down, a shadow in the night, silent and deadly, despite his size. He approached the castle, uncaring who saw him, knowing no one would interfere. He was a dragon king. He took what he wanted.

He aimed for a particular balcony, flaring his wings and letting it slow his descent. He shifted as he fell, smoke pulling the scales from his flesh and reshaping his bones. The pain was pleasure, a release as his body popped back into place. When the smoke dissipated into the night, he was a man again, pale skin bright in the night, crouched low and predatory on the banister. He slowly unfolded himself, stepping down onto the balcony, and stalked to the doors.

One was left ajar, and he silently pushed it open, just enough to slip his body through.

The room was dark, save for slivers of light that fell through the windows. His eyes adjusted easily, focusing in on the still form on the bed, curled beneath the blankets. Arulean stalked across the room on silent feet, body swaying and warmth coiling low in his gut as he surveyed his prize, his prey, his lover, his omega.

Black, wavy hair was strewn out across the pillows, his face turned away from Arulean and relaxed in sleep. He felt a small smile curl his lips as he gently lifted the blankets at the edge of the bed, slipping beneath them. Rajiah stirred as his weight pressed into the bed, but he settled down quickly. Arulean slid closer, pressing his body up against Rajiah's back, wrapping one arm around his waist while the other slid beneath his neck.

He pressed his lips to the back of Rajiah's neck, running his tongue along the bumps of his spine, tasting the salt of his skin. He slept with nothing on, and his flesh was warm against Arulean's, chilled from the night. He was already somewhat hard from his thoughts and anticipation, and he pressed his length against the curve of Rajiah's ass.

The omega stirred again. Arulean pressed his lips to his neck, nipping and licking and sucking along the curve of it, from his ear to his shoulder. The man tilted his head, breathing heavily as he gave Arulean more room. The alpha's hands roamed over his chest, his stomach, his thighs, teasing the dark curls but dancing around the thickening cock of the omega. He pinched his nipple, rolling the bud between two fingers, and Rajiah gasped softly, arching back into Arulean's chest. He chuckled, the sound rumbling deep in his throat. He could smell Rajiah's scent getting stronger in his arousal, and he playfully nosed the skin above his scent glands, breathing him in and letting out a shuddering breath. He had the sweetest scent he had ever come across.

Unable to wait much longer, driven by desire, need, and a primal hunger that he couldn't keep at bay, his hand slipped around the curve of Rajiah's hip, around the curve of one cheek to dip into the cleft of his ass. He prodded the entrance there, teasing it and rubbing with his fingers. He could feel the moisture building, arousal already making the omega wet. When he pushed in a finger, Rajiah's spine arched again, a soft gasp and a moan escaping his lips.

"A-Arulean?" Came the soft inquiry, breathless and perfect.

Arulean hummed against his skin, nosing his way up Rajiah's neck. "Rajiah," He breathed into his ear, enjoying the feeling of the omega shivering against him. "Rajiah, I want you." He whispered, rocking his hips forward and pressing himself against him.

Rajiah arched his back, pressing his ass against him, exposing more of his neck. "Please..." Came the breathy reply.

That was all Arulean needed to continue. He pressed his finger deeper into the omega, turning his wrist to quirk the finger, exploring and finding all the spots that make him gasp and moan. He added a second, stretching him out before adding a third. Rajiah took him in easily, hips moving in encouragement and delicious sounds dropping from his lips.

"Arulean... Arulean, please..."

He pulled his fingers out, rolling on top of him. "Hold onto me, my love..." He whispered against his lips, and Rajiah obeyed without hesitation, wrapping his legs around his hips and his arms around his neck. Arulean pushed into him, and he kissed him, swallowing the whimpers as he stretched the omega. He was warm and wet, and it felt like heaven. It drove him wild with hunger and need. He stayed still only long enough for them both to adjust before he pulled back slowly and snapped his hips forward. Rajiah gasped before letting loose a long, drawn out moan, keening when Arulean did it again.

Rajiah was beautiful in the slivers of starlight, lighting up his dark skin and glimmering in his dark eyes. He was beautiful, lips parted, moisture gleaming on them. He was beautiful, noises and gasps and whines dropping from his lips like he couldn't contain them. Arulean loved them. He loved the sounds, each and every one. He loved how loud he was and how he didn't hold back. He loved how Rajiah moved with him, unable to keep his hips still. He loved how he writhed beneath him, legs quivering and hands constantly groping, nails biting his skin and stinging his flesh. He loved that he bit at his shoulder and his lips, loved how his tongue pushed into Arulean's mouth with force, fingers in his hair holding him still as the omega claimed him. He loved how he felt, hot and wet everywhere they touched, driving him quickly to his climax.

He was beginning to realize he loved a lot of things about Rajiah Bronze, but more than anything, he was pretty sure he simply loved him.

He didn't knot him. He knew he couldn't. Not if he wanted his bond with Lyphnia to be strong enough to bring her down, pull her leash tight, and keep her from causing mayhem. He couldn't mate with Rajiah the way he wanted to, but that wouldn't stop him from claiming the omega as his own.

And claim him, he did. He marked him everywhere hands and teeth could reach, just as Rajiah claimed him in return. He pounded him into the mattress again and again, bringing them both to orgasm several times, and making a mess of the sheets. And when he could no longer move, he laid on his back, attempting to catch his breath, before Rajiah, his beautiful, young, vibrant omega, mounted him and rode him, hips twitching and rolling as he brought them to orgasm one last time before collapsing on top of him.

With them both breathless, sweaty, sore, and unable to move, he stayed inside Rajiah. They weren't knotted, but at that moment, he could pretend they were. He closed his eyes, running a hand up and down the man's back while the other gently ran fingers through his hair. They kissed sweet and languid until even the effort of holding up their heads was too much. Rajiah fell asleep first, nuzzled and tucked under his chin, body curled up on his chest.

Arulean let sleep take him slowly, sinking into unconsciousness with the thought that he never wanted this feeling to fade, and he never wanted to let Rajiah go.

CHAPTER
TWELVE

Arulean was tired. He was emotionally and physically drained. And yet, as he stood on the balcony of his study, overlooking the valley and the dragons that flew above, his heart felt light, a weight that had been pulling him into the earth had been lifted. For the first time in years, he was able to breathe easy, knowing that he had done something to help his people.

The Final Meeting had been long and gruelling. It had started much as he expected it to, with Lyphnia sweeping into the council room with a flourish and taking her seat like her victory was ensured. She hadn't been expecting Arulean's retaliation when she brought up war again, and he couldn't quite blame her for that. He had been passive for far too long and allowed her to test the boundaries.

It was during that meeting when he had taken Rajiah's advice and tightened her leash, using their mateship bond, forced and strengthened through centuries, to keep her in check. He used everything at his disposal to force her into submission: his aura flaring, his scent strong, his harsh voice, and unwavering cold eyes. He tore into her with his words, cutting through her arguments, making her look like a petulant and bitter child, making the council question her logic when she proposed no more hiding, making them question her leadership. He brought up the past, how following her had led to folly. And, throughout it all, he pressed on her from all sides with his aura, an aura that he hadn't utilized to its full potential in centuries.

He showed them that he was still as powerful as he used to

be, and he showed them why he had remained a dragon king for so long. Lyphnia was powerful on her own, but a lot of her influence had been gained through her mateship with him. He, on the other hand, had gained his position on his own, and he could stand on his own, with or without her.

She had been forced to submit, to bite back her words, though he could see the rage swirling in her eyes, in her aura, smell it in her scent. She wasn't happy. She was seething. But there was nothing she could do about it. Arulean had won, again, and she knew it.

With her foundation weakened and her position shaken, it was easy for Arulean to make his case for the Paranormal Pact. It was easy to weave his words, use his influence, and show them the confidence needed to get them on his side. He didn't use his aura to force them to submit as he had with Lyphnia, but it felt like he had. He had given them barely any room for contradiction, and none of them argued against him. Not without Lyphnia as their spear head.

And so The Summit concluded with the decision to tentatively enter the Paranormal Pact, to keep hidden and secret until their people, hopefully, faded from knowledge into myth in the minds of humans. They made the announcement, and not everyone was happy, but there was little they could do. Arulean knew he couldn't please everyone, but he could do what he believed was best for his people. He made it clear that they were to remain hidden and under no circumstances engage in combat with humans, and that anyone who did so would not receive support from the rest of their kind. He said this with a pointed look at Lyphnia, who scowled and looked away.

Arulean felt powerful again. He felt influential. He felt like a king in more than just name. He felt like someone his people could turn to. It made him feel lighter and more solid. Made him feel alive. He had been fading into a ghost of his former self, retreating into a shell without realizing it. Gerrald had tried to get him to understand, but it had been to no avail. And then Rajiah came crashing into his life and ripped him from his shell, pulled him back into reality and forced him to face the world and himself. And he came out stronger for it. All because of him.

The Summit had officially concluded two days ago, and they had gone on the last flight the night before. It had been much more invigorating than the first. Arulean had truly felt alive and less like he was simply going through the motions. He and Lyphnia had led the flight, as was tradition, but the emotional gap between them was wider and deeper than ever. They spun around each other, circling high above the valley as far from each other as they could get. They were two powerful figureheads, tied together but no longer lovers. No longer friends. He had severed that connection for good when he humiliated her at the Final Meeting in front of the council, but he couldn't bring himself to regret it.

The valley and the skies above the mountains had been alive with dragons, and it had warmed his heart. They were so few compared to what they had once been, but they were still there, still alive, still fighting, still surviving. They had taken a heavy hit centuries ago, but they would come back. They were dragons, and they were strong. He reveled in watching them dart and fly around each other and with each other over the valley. He loved watching the cacophony of scales and bodies, writhing in the air, living, breathing, and joining in a flight that was filled with kinship. He overlooked them all from his position high above them, watching over them with a proud and gentle eye.

He watched Rajiah. He watched as the omega led another fruitless chase for the alphas. He knew that the omega wouldn't let any of them catch him. He felt a rumbling of envy in his chest, but he smothered it down, knowing the man still bore his mark and his scent. He was his, even if he couldn't make him his mate. So he let Rajiah have his fun and put on his show, both of them knowing Arulean would come to claim him later that night.

And now, as Arulean watched over the valley, dragons filtered out of it. Most of them left in their dragon forms, and would no doubt remain so until they neared human civilization, or remain flying high enough to avoid being spotted, or just avoid humans altogether. With The Summit over, they would all return to their homes or whatever they were doing prior to the call. They would go back to surviving, go back to living. Arulean found the sight of them, all proud and strong in their glory, scales glinting in the sun and shining through their wings, a bitter sweet sight. He was proud of his people. He loved them, but he was sad to see them go.

Dragons did not live as other shifters did. They didn't live in packs. They lived separately and came together on rare occurrences. And Arulean was starting to think that was a fairly lonely existence.

"I will be leaving on the morrow."

Her voice came soft but sharp, cutting through his thoughts and the bubble of his tranquility. He hadn't heard or felt her approach. Or perhaps he did, but he hadn't thought to dwell on it. He had grown so used to her presence over the years.

He took a step back to turn, hands clasped behind his back. She stood behind him, in the open doorway to his study. Her hair was loose, falling down her back in silky, blood red curls. Her eyes were lined, make-up perfect, showing off her flawless features. Her lips, painted red, were pressed into a thin, expressionless line that was unlike her. Her eyes were dark, glinting red where the irises caught the light. She gazed at him steadily, and he gazed back. Silence stretched between them, a breeze billowing their hair as their bodies stood frozen.

He could not say he was surprised she was leaving. On some level, he had expected it. After he had humiliated her and abashed her like a child in the Final Meeting, pushing his presence over her until she submitted, he knew she would leave. They would still be bound by their mateship. That was not so easily broken. But he knew she wouldn't want to be near him, living with him, when he could so easily suppress her like that. When he had made a fool of her in front of their peers.

"Where will you go?" He asked, finally breaking the silence.

She managed a nonchalant shrug, putting one hand on her hip. "I have an idea of lands I want to scout out, build a home. Something grander than this place. Some place where dragons are welcome."

He raised an eyebrow. "Lands void of humans, I hope." He said, voice low and even.

She sneered. "Yes, Arulean, lands free of humans. I will abide by your Pact for now, but do not think I have given up what I believe is right, what we deserve."

He cocked a wry smile. "I would not dream of it. You are a strong woman, Lyphnia. A strong dragon. I wish we could be on the same side."

She sighed then, a small exhale through her nose. "As do I, Arulean. Perhaps, one day, we can be again."

"Perhaps." He doubted it, but there was no harm in humoring her.

Her eyes flickered to his neck, where he had several marks that were clear and on display. He hadn't bothered trying to hide them, nor had he scrubbed Rajiah's scent from his body. "I do not suppose you will release me from our mateship?"

"You know I will not. Friends or enemies, our bond is important to our people."

"Even if it is clear that you desire another?"

He nodded sharply. "Even if that is the case, yes."

"I suppose this means I can take a lover or two without your interference?"

Something rose in him, something predatory and possessive, something old and ancient. It died down quickly. He had Rajiah. "That is what it means, yes."

"But you will not make him your mate in truth?"

"I will not."

She hummed. "He will not like that."

"Keeping our bond is more important."

"To you, perhaps." She looked him over, eyes calculating. "Perhaps one day you will change your mind."

"Perhaps."

They lapsed back into silence, each quietly appraising the other. There was a world of things left unsaid between them, bridges that had been burned and things that needed closure.

And yet, when it came down to it, they found they had nothing to say to each other at all. The time for that had passed, and the time for separation had been long coming.

She took a step back, eyes on him still. "I suppose this is goodbye then."

He nodded, expression softening. "Goodbye, Lyphnia. May the wind carry you swiftly on your travels."

"I suppose I will see you on the next Blood Moon?"

He nodded. "You will. And every other after that."

She tilted her head to the side, something dark and sorrowful swirling in her eyes, a vulnerability she rarely let show. When she spoke, her voice was softer, with less of an edge. "Do you think we will ever conceive again?"

He gave her a small, honest smile. "We can hope."

She nodded, then turned on her heel, walking briskly across the study without much preamble or lingering. "Goodbye, Arulean." She called, raising a hand to wave over her shoulder. That was Lyphnia. Quick, precise, firm in her decisions. She wasn't one to linger, and not one to allow too much emotion.

He watched her go, letting the closing of the heavy oaken doors resonate around the room. "Goodbye, Lyphnia."

She left the valley in a flourish. Red scales glistening in the mid-afternoon sun, she was bright and vibrant, a streak of blood and fire against the blue sky. She did circles above the valley, and then, with a mighty roar of defiance and freedom, and a mighty down stroke of her wings, she shot out to the southeast, disappearing over the mountaintops. Several other dragons followed her, her entourage no doubt, carrying chests of her possessions that she refused to leave behind. She said she would send for others at a later date.

Arulean watched from the ground, standing at the top of the grand staircase that led up to his castle's front doors. He stood tall and regal, clothes simple for his station but fanciful nonetheless. His hands were clasped behind his back, chin lifted to gaze up at the sky. His long, dark hair was swept back and tied at the nape of his neck with a black ribbon. The breeze was cool against his cheeks.

He felt him approach. He felt it with the entirety of his being, smelled his scent on the wind, felt his aura pulsing behind him, heard his light but sure footfalls. It was as if everything in him was reaching out for him, burning at the omega's nearness and begging to be closer.

He stayed where he was. "The others have already left." He said, voice even, conversational. Lyphnia and her entourage were the last to leave, save for Arulean, those who lived here, and Rajiah. He didn't ask, but the question hung in the air between them. Rajiah answered anyway.

"I won't be leaving." He said softly, stopping when he was standing at his side, head tilted up to the sky. They stood close, arms brushing.

"Are you certain?"

"I am."

"I cannot be your mate in truth, Rajiah." He said softly, regret coloring his voice. He closed his eyes, feeling the sun on his face. "I wish I could, but I cannot."

"Will you be my mate in every other sense?" Arulean opened his eyes, turning his head to gaze down at the omega. His head was tilted up, dark eyes on the sky, sun shining on his dark skin, wind in his loose, wavy hair. "Will you be mine?"

His lips quirked into a small, earnest smile, gaze softening. "I already am. I am here, as I am, as strong as I am, because of you. You make me feel alive, Rajiah. You have my heart."

He breathed out a small sigh, finally turning his gaze to Arulean's. He felt a shiver as their eyes locked, amazed at all the warmth and fire those amber eyes held. "And you have mine, Arulean." He tilted his head to the side, smile widening as he laid a hand on Arulean's arm. "I'm proud of you, for everything, for standing up for everyone, for being the light we need."

He laid his hand over Rajiah's. "I could not have done it without you. Everything I have to give is yours. Everything I am is yours."

Rajiah's grin was blinding. He leaned into Arulean, and the alpha laid an arm across his shoulders, pulling him into his side. Rajiah melted against him, smaller arms wrapping around his waist. "I never had a home..." He said, voice soft and content. "I always wandered, and I didn't really think I needed a home. But now... I think I've found my home with you. I want you to be my home."

Arulean's arm around him tightened as he said softly, "Perhaps with you around, this castle will finally feel like a home again."

Together they turned, heading back toward the castle doors wrapped tightly together. They had a lot of work ahead of them. Lyphnia's things would need to be gathered and prepared to move, and they would move Rajiah into Arulean's room. He still had messages to answer and messages to send, informing the other paranormal communities and other shifters of the dragons joining the Paranormal Pact. He had a lot of planning to do. He had a valley and a village of shifters to take care of, to make sure were doing alright and would do alright come winter.

But for now, he was content to simply bask in Rajiah's warmth.

"We should invite the villagers to the castle." He said suddenly.

Arulean raised an eyebrow, glancing down at him. "Oh?"

Rajiah nodded, smirking up at him, a little shyly. "Yeah, when was the last time the villagers were allowed to freely visit the castle?"

He thought about that. "Never, I do not think."

"Then it's a perfect time to start. Let them meet you, the man who protects them. Regge and Marli want to meet you officially, and that werewolf pack we helped have been eager to see you again. Whether you realize it or not, Arulean, you're their hero. Everyone in this valley, shifters great and small look up to you. You're their leader." His smile curved wider, a mischievous glint in his eyes. "You're like the Alpha of this pack. This giant, mismatched pack of shifters who just want to live together peacefully. Shifters of all kinds who just came together to live under your guiding leadership."

He had never thought of it like that before. He had founded the valley as a safe haven from humans, but he hadn't ever thought of the citizens who came to the valley as a pack. But that was honestly what it seemed like. A whole civilization of shifters from all backgrounds, coming together and combining to make one large pack that lived under his rule. He had been so busy focusing on the problems of the dragons that he hadn't quite thought about everyone else who looked up to him as well. Rajiah helped him see that.

If we can't protect those weaker than us, then what good are we?

"One large pack, hmm?" He said, a small smile forming. "I like the sound of that."

Rajiah smirked, nuzzling into Arulean's side, arms tightening around his waist. "I thought you might... I was thinking we could call ourselves the Shadow Pack."

He paused just outside the doors to the castle, turning to face Rajiah. He was close, his warm, sweet scent wrapping around him, marking his skin and clothes. He loved the omega's scent. He loved him. He raised an eyebrow, ghost of a smile on his lips. "The Shadow Pack?"

Rajiah was grinning, eyes lighting up and crinkling at the corners. "Yeah, because you're all dark like a shadow, the shadow that watches over us. But also, because our pack will be dedicated to keeping shifters safe and hidden from humans. A shadow."

He chuckled softly, leaning forward until his forehead was pressed to Rajiah's. "Our pack. The Shadow Pack. I like that." He breathed. "No matter where we go, or where we settle, we can offer others a safe place to live."

Rajiah's smile softened, leaning into Arulean's touch. He snaked his arms around his neck. "That sounds perfect." He breathed, eyes half lidded and lips parted. "Kiss me?"

And he did. He wrapped Rajiah up in his arms and pulled him tight, lips slow and languid as they tasted each other, bodies melding into one. His heart pounded in his chest, his head dizzy, his limbs light, his stomach fluttering. Their future was uncertain, as all futures were. But there was one thing Arulean knew with the upmost certainty: he loved this man, and he would do anything and everything to keep him at his side.

"I love you," He murmured against his lips.

Rajiah chuckled, the sound low and sweet, making the happiness in his chest bubble and pop. "I love you, too, you big idiot."

Arulean pulled back just a little, enough to give Rajiah a puzzled and amused look. "I do not think anyone has ever had the audacity to call me an idiot."

Rajiah's grin was like the sun. "Well, get used to it. Cause I'm not going anywhere for a long, long time."

He liked the sound of that.

The end.

Manufactured by Amazon.ca
Bolton, ON